HIDDEN DEPTHS

Published by Rily Publications Ltd, 2020
ISBN 978-1-84967-412-6
Copyright © Ifan Morgan Jones, 2020

The Quick Reads project in Wales is an initiative coordinated by the
Books Council of Wales and supported by the Welsh Government.
Printed and bound by CPI Group (UK) Ltd, Croydon, CR0 4YY

Cover design by Tanwen Haf

CYNGOR LLYFRAU CYMRU
BOOKS COUNCIL of WALES

HIDDEN DEPTHS

IFAN MORGAN JONES

PROLOGUE

THE LOST CITY

'Did you ever hear the legend of Cantref Gwaelod?'

I jumped. I'd thought I was on my own on the grey sand of the beach. I'd snuck out without anyone noticing, having taken my school stuff out of my bag and filling it with sweets and crisps. Enough to keep me going for a day or two, I'd thought.

I hadn't intended to go very far. Just disappear long enough to make everyone worry. Make my foster parents and teachers apologise for being so impatient, and then everything would be OK again.

Now I was here, shivering in the dark and cold, listening to the crash of the waves and eating a packet of crisps. And someone else was there with me. A stranger. I turned to look and saw he was standing about ten feet behind me. I couldn't see his face in the darkness, but he was definitely talking to me. There was no one else around.

'This entire part of the bay used to be above the land,' the man said, his deep voice rolling across the beach like the crash of a wave. He swept his arm across the wide expanse of the slate-dark sea. The sky had been the colour of porridge all day but now it was opening up and the moon's rays twinkled on the water. 'Do you see those trunks over there?'

I looked over. The waves were beating up against what I'd thought were dark, pointed stones at the water's edge, but now could see were the blackened skeletons of tree roots.

I craned my head back to look at him. He had a mossy beard, cheekbones as high as cliff faces and the light of the moon twinkled in a pair of friendly eyes. 'Are you a teacher?' I asked.

I didn't want to make friends with a teacher. I was unpopular enough with the other children due to my too-short trousers and supermarket daps. The only reason I hadn't been bullied yet was because I was too invisible for anyone to take any notice of me. Perhaps my foster carers had phoned someone from the school to come and talk to me?

'I'm not a teacher, but I know some history,' the man said cheerfully. 'Those are 6,000 years old.' He pointed at the tree-trunks. 'Can you believe that? Tree-trunks older than before the Egyptians built the Pyramids. Right here on our beach in Wales.'

That was cool, I had to admit. Since moving here just before the start of the school term (this was my fourth school in six years) I hadn't thought there was anything very interesting about this wind-swept coast of west Wales.

The man fell silent for a while and I got the impression that he wouldn't leave until I said something. I hastily swallowed the last of my crisps and wiped the crumbs off my mouth with my jumper sleeve. 'So ... what happened? Why did it drown?'

'Well, scientists say the sea rose up when the ice caps melted and flooded the plain,' he answered, pushing his hands into his trouser pockets and jutting out his chin. 'But the legend tells us something else. It says the plain was the kingdom of a king called Gwyddno Garanhir and was hemmed in by huge stone walls on all sides. One day there was a storm and the man in charge of the flood gates on these walls was too busy drinking and partying, so he forgot to close them. The sea came in thick and heavy, and they could no longer close the flood gates. Everyone had to flee, and Cantref Gwaelod was drowned.'

I looked out at the wide, glittering sea and imagined the ruins of the disappeared city beneath the waves. And then I thought about the people leaving. Hundreds, if not thousands of people, climbing like terrified ants up into the hills behind me, scattered across the shore.

'So everyone lost their homes?' My voice trembled as I spoke.

'It's just a legend,' the man said. 'But they say you can still hear the bells of Cantref Gwaelod on a quiet day.'

I listened but could hear nothing but the thrashing

of the waves on the shore and the occasional screech of a far off seagull. A wind came from the west, stinging my cheeks, and I wrapped my arms around myself for warmth. 'So who was supposed to close the doors?'

'His name was Seithenyn.'

'And they blamed him?'

'Well, it was his fault!' The man laughed.

I sat there for a while, my eyes out on the sea but my thoughts drawn inwards, thinking. A breeze washed over me and the smell of seaweed tickled my nose.

'I like Seithenyn,' I said finally.

'You like him?'

'Well, he was the bad guy in the story,' I said. 'But he made one mistake, one easy mistake, and lost everything. And he had to escape from everyone who hated him.' I could taste the bitterness in my own voice. 'Anyone could have noticed that it was stormy and that the doors needed closing. They just blamed him, because they needed someone to blame, to make everything easier on themselves.'

'You're a clever boy,' the man said, finally. 'Most kids – actually most adults – just accept the story they're told. You took it and turned it on its head.'

I'm not clever, I wanted to say. It's just because I know what it's like not to have a home or any friends. And to be the one to blame.

I clenched my fists and the clouds closed in again overhead, cutting off the silver rays on the water. All I could see was a dirty smudge in the sky where the moon should have been. A chill wind blew again and with it came a disturbing new thought.

Why was this man telling me this? Did he know what had happened? Did he know why I didn't have parents, and why I was in Wales? Was he a reporter?

But I didn't say anything, in case he was a reporter.

'Do you believe the story?' I asked, changing the subject.

He shrugged. 'Legends are stories we tell to better understand ourselves. Whether it actually happened, maybe that doesn't matter.'

I thought about that.

'I should go back,' I said. 'Or people will be worried, I suppose.'

'That sounds like a good idea. I'd offer you a lift, but I don't think you would take it.'

'No.'

I heard the man's shoe crunch on the sand as he walked away. Then he stopped.

'Rees?'

'Yes?'

'The people of Cantref Gwaelod lost their home, but they still had each other. If the legend does have a message, it's that your home is where you choose to make it.'

I paused, embarrassed. 'OK.'

He continued walking and disappeared over the top edge of the beach and out of sight. It was freezing. I got up and grabbed my bag, the strap chaffing my cold hand. It was only as I trudged back up the beach that I realised that the man had known my name. Definitely a teacher.

I reached the beach road and turned south towards my foster parents' house, a mile down the road. And suddenly I was bathed in light. I looked up, expecting to see that the moon had come out again. But what I saw I'd never forget.

At first, I thought it was some kind of plane, but it was too bright and round. It shot off overhead and then seemed to plunge down towards the sea. I bared my teeth, expecting a crash, but it disappeared out of sight. The light went out as it hit the dark expanse of the sea, slipping under the waves like an electric manta ray.

For the next twelve years, I told no one about what I'd seen. I didn't *know* what I'd seen. And who would have believed a troubled orphan boy in Asda daps who was always running away from home and getting into trouble, anyway?

CHAPTER 1

THE CALL

Twelve years later and I was ... still running away.

I carefully closed the corrugated iron back door of the homeless shelter behind me and threw the old Adidas carrier bag over my shoulder. I'd thrown everything out that I didn't need and was down to the basics – a one-man tent and sleeping bag, a couple of shirts and a razor so that I didn't look like a total deadbeat if I needed a job, and a pay-as-you-go phone.

It was the early hours of the morning when I made my escape, and only a row of electric street lamps lit up the street outside. Every now and then the wind shook a few more leaves from the trees. To anyone else it may have felt scary and lonely. But I was happy. I felt I could only understand the world by being apart from it, by looking at it from the outside. An alien.

'Rees!'

I could have kept going, pretending not to hear her voice, but I'd already flinched. She'd notice that.

'Rees!' she yelled louder, her voice echoing down the empty street. 'Where ... where are you going?'

I turned and saw her standing at the open door, in just

her vest and pyjama bottoms, bathed in the sterile light of the street lamp. She looked cold and pale, but beautiful.

'I'm moving on, Megan.'

'So. Just like that? You just sneak out? That's – what a shitty thing to do.'

'You know I don't like it here.' The homeless shelter had a 7pm curfew and we slept in bunks, four in a room. If anyone farted in their sleep there was no escaping it – you would smell it all night. Then there were the people on a bad drug trip, babbling, hallucinating. And because some people had 'problems' we were all caged up like inmates at a prison. We couldn't even bring in our own food and drink. 'I'm fed up of being treated like a kid,' I said.

'You're not leaving the shelter, Rees. You're leaving me. Without saying goodbye.' She folded her arms. 'You're such a dick.'

'I never said I'd stick around.'

'I thought you lov— I thought you liked me, at least.'

I wanted her to swear at me and slam the door. To explode. That would have been easier. But she was just standing there, hurt and small, in the stark doorway.

'You can do better than me, Megan. So can everyone.'

'The council won't help you if you walk away again.'

I shook my head. 'I don't want any help.'

A breeze sent the dry autumn leaves scraping across the road. I tried not to look at her.

'Rees —' She stalled. 'I just don't know what you're looking for.' A tear rolled down her cheek. 'What you can't find in here,' she said, raising a finger to her heart, 'you'll never find out there.'

'I'm happy, Megan. I'm happy *alone*. That's why I'm leaving. Bye. And thank— uh, yeah, bye.'

I turned and left her there. I felt her gaze burning the back of my head like red-hot lasers but I refused to look back. I bit my lip. If I just carried on walking it would be fine. She'd soon forget about me. I could walk until morning, lost in my thoughts, or find a place to pitch up. I couldn't hurt anyone if I was alone.

As it was, I didn't get any further than an empty park in the middle of the city. Perhaps I wanted to leave open the option of going back. Back to Megan. Or maybe I just needed to think about what I wanted to do with my life.

There were no street lights here, so I could see the clouds overhead, low and dark, floating like ghostly boats in front of the moon. There were few places that felt as eerie as a playground at night. The swings rocked back and forth. The roundabout spun, creaking.

I walked along the path around the edge of the playing field, before sitting on a bench at the far end. I drew my legs in to avoid the puddle that had collected in a pothole in the tarmac. A child's plastic toy lay at the bottom, glaring up at me with a frozen grin.

I put my head in my hands. What was I doing? What was I always running away from?

'What *are* you always running away from?'

I jumped. 'Who's there?'

'Just someone who wants to help.'

The voice – female – was almost swallowed by the whisper of the wind through the branches of the trees.

'I don't want company,' I said. And how did she know I was running away? Had I said that out loud?

'I think anyone sitting in the dark wants to be found. And anyway, what we want and what we need are different things.'

Then I saw them. Two glowing eyes, like two pools of molten silver, hanging in the trees in front of me. The eyes of a cat or a fox. Something nocturnal and fierce. Did human eyes shine in the dark like that?

'Follow me,' the voice purred.

'Why?'

'Because it's me you've been looking for your whole life.'

I relaxed. A prostitute, I thought. I must have wandered over to a seedier side of the city, although hiding behind some trees in an abandoned park was a strange way of doing business. 'Sorry, but I don't have any money.'

She cackled mockingly.

'Money is of no use where we're going. You are

restless. You sense in the marrow of your bones that you are destined for something greater. You just need to be pointed in the right direction. And I'm here to help you do that.'

Then she – it – stepped out. It wasn't a woman at all. It was a deer! A doe, glowing with a silvery-green light, a light that couldn't be explained by the full moon alone but radiated out through the creature's skin as if some fire burned within it.

I stared open-mouthed. This is a trick, I thought. A prank. A projection. An art installation. Someone was making fun of me. The woman was hiding in the woods somewhere, holding a microphone.

'Very funny. Cut it out.' But I could hear the tremble in my voice.

The deer walked towards me and stuck its snout so close to my face I could feel its cool breath tickle my nose. 'I was going to lead you,' it said. 'But now you'll have to catch me.' It turned and leapt back into the forest.

Was I dreaming? Had someone at the shelter slipped something into my drink? I could feel the cold bite in my fingers. The weight of my shoes on my feet. This was *real*. The humdrum greyness of my life had been peeled back for a moment and I could glimpse ... something behind it. Something otherworldly. Something divine.

I gave chase.

CHAPTER 2

MEMORIES

The ghostly animal tore through the trees. I groped after it, as fast as I could without losing my footing on the mossy ground.

'Wait!' I cried.

I could hear its hooves beating down on the roots and hard earth.

'I can't catch up!'

I leapt over a rotting log and a narrow ditch, and almost lost my balance climbing up a steep bank on the far side. My legs stung with the pounding effort and my cheeks were raw from the scraping of tree branches. Was I still in the middle of the city? I could hear no sounds of traffic and my nose was full of the earthy smell of bracken and peat. I should have been in the outer-Cardiff suburbs by now, but this forest seemed old and endless.

I came to a small clearing and there was the creature, stopped dead. It was hemmed in by an overgrown, crumbling wall too high to leap over. It paced back and forth, silver-green air billowing like geysers from its nostrils.

'Come and get me.'

I approached the creature carefully, arms out wide to prevent its escape.

Why the hell was I doing this?

'You know why,' it said, 'or you wouldn't have chased me this far.'

I leapt, intending to grab the creature around its neck, but missed it by inches as it bounded away.

'You won't get me that easily,' it said, and leapt. And as it hung in the air, it transformed, shrunk, and landed on the side of a tree. It was now a silver squirrel, with little green ears. It turned and gave me a smug grin, before hopping over the top of the wall.

I took a deep, tired breath and picked myself up. Annoyed at myself, annoyed at the creature. My chest was heaving. I should go back, I thought, but I didn't know where back was. And I wanted to know if there was something new at the end of all this. 'Wait!' I scaled the ruined wall and dropped down on the other side.

It was a long way down and I fell and rolled, landing in a pile of rotting autumn leaves. It was as dark as a tar pit down there, the air close and thick. I groped and scrambled through the dense undergrowth and spotted a faint crystal-green light ahead.

'Wait!' I called, stretching out an arm and almost tripping over a rotted tree stump. The creature, still in squirrel form, was stood upright on an old round-backed bridge above a narrow stream. It was poised and still, apart from its tail, which twitched nervously.

I stared, meeting its cold gaze. I felt like I was in a dream and completely awake at the same time.

'Almost there,' the squirrel said. 'Hurry.'

'Where are we going?'

'Deeper.'

Sighing, I bent double with my palms on my knees. 'It's hard work.'

'It's not supposed to be easy.'

'What isn't?' I asked. 'I don't know what you want.'

'As I said, want and need are different things. You must free yourself from the first to embrace the second.'

The squirrel somersaulted off the back of the bridge, transformed into a shining silver fish, hung in mid-air for a second, then landed in the water with a plop. The stream turned a silver-emerald and it shot forward, its tail beating furiously as it propelled itself through the water like a clockwork missile.

I jogged down the side of the river, careful not to turn my ankle on the huge white pebbles, like polished dinosaur eggs, on either side.

At last the forest opened up, where the stream, now a river, ran into boggy ground. The marsh was surrounded by a large cliff face full of crevasses. I suddenly felt as if I was being watched from all sides. The little alcoves on the cliff face had heavy iron gates on them, like the bars of the bunk beds at the homeless shelter.

I couldn't see the fish, or the silvery light. But I could hear a low, sonorous sound that seemed to be rising from the earth, like the glum note of a horn.

'Where am I?' I asked, my heart thudding like a failing engine. 'What do you want with me?'

The despondent note grew higher and became the moaning of a thousand mouths, rising from the boggy ground, and locked behind the iron cages on the cliff side.

'I'd tell you not to be afraid,' she said, her voice seeming to come out of the air. 'But this place is fear. This is the deepest part of your mind, where you have locked away your most painful memories. To be free of them, to settle your wandering spirit, you must face them. Fight them.'

'I don't want to,' I said. I felt like a ten-year-old again. Like a whimpering little boy.

'Want and need are different things.'

I took a deep breath and marched across the boggy ground. And as I walked past the cages with their iron gates I recognised some of those locked within, and heard their voices clearly. Daniel Pitman, the bully who made my life hell at school, calling me Oliver Twist and giving me a dead leg every day. 'Where are your parents?' he rasped now, clutching the bars. Mr Williams, the sadistic gym teacher, who let the other kids use me as a tackle bag during rugby lessons. 'Take your lumps, boy,' he said, grinning in the dark.

And I heard Megan's voice too: 'I thought you lov— I thought you liked me, at least.' An icy hand grabbed my heart and squeezed.

Every cage I passed, every puddle I crossed, had something in it I wanted to forget. People who had hurt me. People who I'd hurt. I didn't know which was worse.

'What's this about?' I asked.

'You want to mean something,' the voice answered, echoing off the cliff walls. 'You want to be someone. Self-sufficient. A hero. Free. But first you need to release yourself from the shackles that bind you.'

'And what are you?'

'I am your inspiration. I am your guide. I am Awen.'

'And what do you —?'

'Tomorrow a man will call at the homeless shelter. He will ask for you. You must not run, you must not refuse. You must go with him.'

'That's it?'

'One more thing. You must never mention me to them, ever. I am our little secret, do you understand?'

Well, why would I want to mention you, I thought. I can't even explain you to myself.

'Good,' she said.

'Wait ... Did you just read my thoughts?'

'I am a function of your mind, as I said. As is all of this.'

'My head is mine!' I raised my hands to my temples. 'I don't want anyone else in there!'

'You're just going to have to share it with me. For a little while.'

I continued walking for what felt like miles, shivering. The voices continued to ring out from the cages on either side. 'I trusted you.' Sonia Williams in Sixth Form, crying after I texted a picture of her undressed to my friends after she dumped me. 'Let go of me!' Ernard Brown whose dense woolly hair I'd made fun of throughout Year Ten. To make myself feel powerful. A cold mist closed around me, and I had to watch my step. I was almost there, I could feel it. At the heart of the corruption, where the rot had started.

And there it was. One final voice – singing. An eerie, ghostly voice. A voice I hadn't heard in years and years. Rising out of the mist.

'Rees! Rees!' it called. 'It's time to come back in for supper. Come on, little monkey.'

A cold sweat broke out on my forehead and my limbs trembled. 'No.'

The voice broke out into song: 'Five little monkeys jumping on the bed, one fell down and bumped his head, Mam called the doctor and the doctor said, "No more little monkeys jumping on the bed!'"

The mist before me cleared. I was standing at the edge of a dark lake, ringed on one side with a dam and a solitary road on the other. A flooded valley in the hills. A valley I'd seen many times as a boy, mostly in my nightmares.

I turned and slipped and scrambled in the dirt. 'No, I can't!'

'Come home, Rees.'

I lost my balance, tripped backwards, and stumbled down the bank before sinking up to my knees into the inky water. I gasped and started up, flailing around for something to hold on to. I felt something grab on to me. Cold, clammy hands. My torso was pulled under, and then my head. My eyes flew open and I looked down and saw their faces. My mother and father and sister, dragging me down.

My mother's mouth opened but no air came out. Just a whisper: 'Come home.'

'Help!' I tried to scream, my words coming out in a rush of bubbles. 'Help me!' I squeezed my eyes shut and thrashed about. Another roaring rush of bubbles and strong, grasping hands, pulling me down, down, down.

I opened my eyes.

I was sitting on the bench, in the park where I'd first heard the voice. What the hell? The park was silent apart from the rasp of the metal chains on the swings and the gush of wind through the tree branches.

Had I just had an extremely weird dream? Was I going crazy?

I looked around, but couldn't see the silvery light, couldn't hear the voice.

I grabbed my bag and ran back to the shelter as fast as I could.

CHAPTER 3

THE STONE CIRCLE

I woke up with a start as a pair of arms grabbed me around my head.

'Rees!'

My first instinct was to wrestle them off, thinking someone was trying to steal my things. Sleeping rough for so many years meant that I'd developed the uncanny ability of going from sleep to full fight or flight in seconds. I looked up and saw Megan's face beaming down at me.

'I knew you'd come back, you dick!' she said, planting her upside-down lips firmly on mine. She squinted with concern. 'Are you OK? You're pale.'

'I'm great,' I said, smiling. 'Am I glad to see you!'

'You are?'

'I just needed time to think, that's all.'

'I didn't sleep at all last night because of your thinking.' She kissed my cheek and my nose.

Whatever had happened last night, whether it was a nightmare or not, had shaken me to my very core. I gave in to the warm caress of her lips.

'Hey, you two, there are other people in this dorm,' came a gruff but sleepy voice from one of the other bunkbeds. 'If you want to cop off, go behind the shed with the rest of them!'

There were guffaws from the other bunks. I raised my head from the pillow. The strip lights had been turned on, but it was still dark outside. Breakfast at the homeless shelter was very early, around 6am, and we had to be out on the street by 7am. Megan had wanted us to get a permanent room, just for the two of us, but that required three months of sticking to all the curfews and rules, and there was a long list of them. As if.

We went through for breakfast in the canteen. Toast and soggy cereal in Tupperware boxes, donated by the local food bank. Plastic tables covered in chequered lino and walls painted pea-soup green. A wooden crucifix hung on the wall.

Megan and I walked in hand in hand like besotted teenagers. I felt guilty. If I hadn't met that ... thing last night, I might be half-way to Land's End or John o'Groats by now.

I knew Megan had been through a lot, with an abusive father, then a string of abusive boyfriends. And me – I just broke her heart rather than her bones. And that was why I'd wanted to get away. The longer I stayed, playing happy families, the more I'd hurt her when I left.

'What are you thinking about now?' Megan asked.

'You.' I smiled.

She smiled back but her eyes were full of concern. 'I don't like when your face goes like that, when you're far away. I want you to be here with me.'

The little tea hatch at the far end of the room slid open. 'Rees,' a voice rang out. It was the shelter manager, Mr Midgley.

'Here we go,' I said to Megan. 'Curfew violation.' I squeezed her leg as I got up.

'Just say you went out for a smoke and got locked out,' she said. 'You were back in your bed by this morning.'

I opened the canteen's side door and looked in at the manager, who was filling out paperwork while three volunteers busied themselves with the dishes behind him. 'Y'alright, Midge?'

He glanced up at me over his receipts. He had a tanned, thick, jowly face and watery, kind eyes. 'There's a bloke outside wanting to see you.'

I paused. 'Police?'

He gave me a look. 'If police, you know the rules.' If I'd committed a crime while staying there, I'd be out on the street. 'He said he'd wait at the stone circle across the street.'

'The circle?'

'I said you was having your breakfast. He said he'd wait. Looked an odd sort of fellow. Smart. Like one of them Jehovah people who go door to door rather than police.' He leant towards me. 'You in any trouble, Rees?'

'Not that I know of,' I said, turning for the door.

Police don't usually wait for you, I thought. Then a shudder went down my spine as I remembered what that mysterious, silver creature had told me.

'Tomorrow a man will call at the homeless shelter. He will ask for you. You must not run, you must not refuse. You must go with him.'

Must be a coincidence, I thought. That had just been a bad nightmare. A minor psychotic episode. Not unusual when you're living rough and under stress.

But I made a decision: whatever this guy offered me, I would refuse. I'd keep my head down at the shelter, with Megan, and try to make the best of things.

Biting my lip, I opened the front door and looked out into the cold, bright autumn morning. Cardiff, with its leafy parks and Victorian terraced houses, looked like it was built for autumn.

The area around the stone circle was mostly empty other than the usual joggers and dog-walkers, but I saw the man straight away. He wore a dark suit, a white shirt and black tie. He looked like an American secret service agent. Only the sunglasses and earpieces were missing. He was standing on the big rock in the middle of the stone circle with his hands on his hips. I approached slowly, attempting to appear as unflustered as possible while trying to imagine what I could possibly have done wrong.

'Hi!' I said.

He hopped off the stone and reached his hand out to shake mine heartily. 'It's nice to meet you again.'

'Again?' I asked, frowning.

'You don't remember me? Well, it has been quite a few years. You can call me Hatch. Come and sit down.' He beckoned me to join him on the big rock in the middle of the stone circle. He did look familiar, but I couldn't quite place him. He had a neatly-trimmed beard and a high, angular face that looked like it should be cast in marble.

I sat on the rock. I'd seen a few of these stone ruins dotted around Wales. A circle of little pointy stones jutting out of the ground and a big, flat one in the middle. There were two or three in Cardiff itself. But I'd never really considered what they were there for. Something to do with old druidic rituals, I'd thought.

'Have I done something wrong?' I asked.

'No, no,' he said. 'I'm actually here to offer you a job.' He had a Welsh accent, but with a twang I couldn't quite place. Probably from the north.

I sat down on the centre stone. 'Before we begin, you should know something. I have to stay out of trouble. The homeless shelter —'

'Oh, don't worry.' He raised an arched eyebrow. 'What we do is beyond the realms of law and order.'

'Well, I've heard that before, but I still did the time.'

He paused and looked at me intently. 'We want to offer you a chance, Rees. An opportunity for a new, exciting life in a city far from here.'

'Where?'

He tapped his foot on the stone. 'You wouldn't believe me if I told you, so I'm going to have to show you.' He took a device from his pocket. It looked like some kind of tablet computer. He began prodding it.

'Well, I think you've got the wrong guy,' I said. 'Uh, I haven't worked for years.'

'A creative incubation period,' he said, tapping away. 'But it suits us fine. We specifically recruit those who have little to leave behind. Men and women who are happy to turn their backs on their lives to follow the uncertainty of their own unique path.'

'Actually, I do have a girlfriend ...'

'Well, you can visit her on your holidays. I'd get up if I were you.'

'Why?'

'Because you're sitting on my ship.'

The stone under my backside suddenly vibrated like an electric toothbrush, and I jumped off. And right then the circle began to spin, slowly at first and then like a whirlpool, faster and faster, until I couldn't make out any individual stone. And as this happened the centre of the circle opened up like a huge sliding door to reveal a floating ship, coarse as stone and marked with etchings and circles. The ship rose up a few metres out of the hole, scattering the last of the autumn leaves that had been sucked into its vortex.

'What the f***k is that?' I asked, my eyes bulging. I looked around to see if anyone else was seeing what I was seeing, but the park seemed empty.

'A *chwyrligwgan*,' Hatch said.

'A twirly-what-what?'

'You're about to go on the journey of a lifetime, Rees,' Hatch said. 'You've never seen eye to eye with the world. Well, good news.' He clapped an arm on my back. 'Everything you thought you knew about how the world worked is wrong.'

The ship spun down and came to rest in front of me, hovering over the grass. It was roughly six feet in height, perhaps twelve in diameter. Hatch touched another button on his tablet and the entrance door slid open.

'Get in,' he said. 'Don't worry, she's bigger on the inside than she looks on the outside.'

'Like the Tardis in *Dr Who*?' I asked, my heart in my throat.

'Um, well, not that big. But if you lie down you won't hit your head.'

I swallowed hard. This was even stranger than the night before. I was definitely going crazy.

CHAPTER 4

CANTREF GWAELOD

Although the ship seemed as dense and rough as a stone from the outside, it was completely different on the inside. The walls were thin and translucent. I could see everything around us in every direction.

Hatch climbed in and lay down next to me. Then he began prodding the ceiling of the craft, calling up different menus which appeared like stickers on the see-through shell.

'Seatbelts on,' he said, pulling a long black strap out of the floor and across his chest. 'Only until we're underwater.'

'The water?' I yanked the straps across my own chest.

'Yes, the *chwyrligwgan* is a submarine more than a spaceship. Don't worry, it can withstand pressure up to 6,000 fathoms.'

I really didn't like going underwater. Not since ... the accident. But I wasn't sure if mentioning that would do me any good right now.

Hatch pressed another button, and the ship was thrown into the air like a pancake from a frying pan. My stomach was left some distance behind us. At first all I could see was blue sky, but then the ship flipped like a coin and I was looking down at the streets of Cardiff.

'Can't people see us?' I shouted.

'Only if we want to be seen,' said Hatch. 'This ship is like an octopus. It can change the colour of its outer shell.'

We were clearly travelling at some speed because the Cardiff suburbs quickly gave way to the outskirts of Caerphilly, and then we were shooting up the Taff Valley and over the yellow-green hills of the Brecon Beacons.

'We'll hit the water in a minute now.'

'Oh God.'

We gained altitude and I could see the rugged edge of the west Wales coast and soon there were two blue stripes visible, rather than one, one of which was darker than the other. The sea was above and the sky underneath, and the ship turned again on its axis, diving down faster and faster.

I felt the skin on my face cling tighter to my skull. We were falling straight as a rock. I wanted to scream out to Hatch that he was going to kill us both. But he looked completely calm.

We hit the sea, sliding in without a sound or a ripple. Everything was dark, except for the occasional flutter of light from the surface of the sea, like blue curtains caught in the wind.

'Better put the headlights on,' Hatch said.

He pressed a button and the sea floor was illuminated all around us. As I stared open-mouthed at the jagged landscape, a jellyfish blobbed past the window. We scooted onwards down a canyon covered in fuzzy plankton and then dipped into a cave.

'Where are we going?' I asked.

He turned and gave me a sly smile. 'So, tell me, Rees, did you ever hear the legend of Cantref Gwaelod?'

'Cantref Gwaelod!' I said, remembering the rolling dark waves and sea spray from that cold night on the beach so many years ago. 'Was – was that you?'

I saw something approaching. At first I thought it was a cliff face, glittering like a diamond. But it was a building covered in thousands of small glass windows – a skyscraper, built completely underwater. And it wasn't the only building either – there were hundreds of them. A vast forest of underwater skyscrapers, some rising from the bottom of the sea, others hanging like stalactites from the roof of this gigantic cave. They were all connected by a network of web-like glass bridges. The submarine plunged between them and I could see tiny people everywhere I looked.

'This is impossible,' I said. 'You could never keep this place secret.'

'Who would ever know we're here?' Hatch asked. 'We are the world's blind spot. A lighthouse on a stormy sea keeping humanity from the rocks.'

The ship swerved dangerously close to one of the buildings and I braced myself for impact but then a gate slid open and the submarine powered through. We were in a long, light tunnel that led further into the heart of the city.

'You're here today because you wanted a new challenge,' Hatch said, in his deep, booming voice. 'Because you felt that the outside world does not see your potential! But here, my friend, you will be appreciated as part of the whole. This is a city where everyone is working towards a common goal of protecting the Earth and humanity.'

Suddenly the view either side was obscured by bubbles. The ship was now rising, and the waters around it cascaded from the hull.

'Here, you'll never feel alone because you're different,' Hatch continued, looking at me with his keen, sparkling eyes. 'At Cantref Gwaelod, everyone is different and that difference is what drives us to achieve miracles, here in our submerged city.' The last of the water flowed from the top of the ship as it rose from the diving port. The door opened and Hatch unfastened his straps and jumped out.

'Keep up now!'

I followed him, shielding my eyes from the blinding brightness. We were in a huge hangar stretching half a mile in either direction, containing hundreds of different ships. There were tens of smaller submarines like the one I'd arrived in, but also many larger ones. One was as tall as a house and as long as a train – it looked as if it could comfortably house a hundred people.

I could see engineers repairing the ships, pilots flying them in and out of the dive ports and other workers walking from place to place, holding the same kind of tablet device Hatch had used.

'They were all recruited, just like you,' he said.

'Do I get a choice in all of this?' I asked. 'What if I don't like it here?'

'Don't worry – no one is kept here against their will. You're always free to leave … though nearly everyone who comes here stays.' He looked at me, shrewdly, with an eyebrow cocked. 'Mind you, we'd have to make sure you didn't tell anyone about us. Cantref Gwaelod is too important for the future of humanity.'

We were heading towards the far end of the room. People skidded by on electric scooters, hurrying to get to their ships. A clash of gossip, shouts, ships taking off and diving pools opening echoed throughout the massive hall.

Then I realised something. No one around me seemed

to be speaking English.

'Wait a second, is everyone here speaking ... Welsh?'

'Yes. The official language of Cantref Gwaelod is Welsh. It always has been.'

'Welsh?' A shiver went down my back as I remembered my less than successful attempts to catch up with the language at school. After a year or two I'd given up completely. 'You guys control the world – in Welsh?'

'Why not? We've been doing it for thousands of years.'

'But ... I can't speak it!'

'Oh, don't worry. You can use a chip until the neural pathways form.' He took out his tablet. 'Could you turn a little bit? I need to get just above your left ear.'

'What?' I veered my head away as he started poking his tablet against my hair.

'Just there. That's where the languages live. Stay still for a second.' I felt a sudden shooting pain in the side of my head as if I'd been injected with a needle.

'Ow!'

'Hwnna'n well?' / 'Is that better?'

'Ydi.' / 'Yes,' I said. *'Dal funud, dwi'n gallu siarad Cymraeg!'* / 'Hang on a second, I can speak Welsh!'

I listened out in amazement – everything that was being said around me now made sense, as if someone had tuned a garbled radio frequency.

'That's amazing,' I said, rubbing my jaw. 'Do you have

any others in there? Megan would love it if I could speak French.'

'There are a few on the menu.' He waved the device. 'Speaking of which, I have a birthday present for you.'

'Birthday? But my birthday is on 22 April.'

'We celebrate our birthdays here on the day we arrived for the first time. Because when we reach Cantref Gwaelod our lives really begin.' Hatch beamed. 'And this is your birthday gift.'

He handed me the tablet. I took it and turned it over in my hands.

'But this is yours.'

'I have plenty of others, this is yours – your key to every door in Cantref Gwaelod. It will mark everything in your diary, giving you access to every laboratory, toilet, and restaurant. You'll use it to send messages to your friends and colleagues, to order food, to play games in your spare time. It'll implant information chips into your brain as required. You'll do everything on and with your Slate.'

I tapped the screen and it lit up. A robotic voice said, in Welsh: 'Good evening, Rees. What would you like to do today?'

'But you must not break any rules,' said Hatch. 'Or you will lose the ability to use your Slate.'

'What kind of rules?' I didn't like the sound of that. It sounded too much like being back at the shelter.

'They're on your Slate. Obvious things like fighting with colleagues, leaving an airlock open and drowning us all, letting a flesh-eating virus loose from the labs – that's very specific because it happened once – not returning a library book. Little things like that.'

By now we had reached the far end of the huge room. Hatch waved his own Slate in front of a grey screen next to the door.

'Open-sesame,' he said.

'You have to say open-sesame?'

Hatch smiled. 'No, but I like to say it.' He pointed out through the door. 'This is the main road through Cantref Gwaelod.'

My eyes opened like saucers as I walked out of the hanger and into the next room. It was a large domed chamber encased in glass, beyond which I could see the underwater kingdom twinkling all around me. At the centre of the dome stood a statue of a fierce-looking man in armour embroidered with Celtic knots. At his feet was carved the motto:

Tra môr yn fur
(*While the sea remains a barricade*)

This seemed to be a central meeting place as there were hundreds of people here – some on foot, others whizzing by on their scooters.

'Who's that?'

'Gwyddno Garanhir, the leader of Cantref Gwaelod.'

I shook my head. 'I feel like I'm going mad.'

'It takes people a few days to adjust,' Hatch said. 'But there's even more to take in – and perhaps it's better to do so all at once.'

'But why have you chosen me?' I felt as if I was riding a wave and was going to crash on the rocks any second. 'No one has ever seen any potential in me before.'

'Wrong – you've never seen any potential in *yourself*. The two things are quite different. And this is the room where you'll be doing all your work.'

A large door loomed over us, with nine letters printed on it: 'The Garden.'

CHAPTER 5

THE CRASH

Unlike the other metal or plastic doors I'd seen along the corridor, this one was made of dark oak, as if it were part of some old castle.

'You need your Slate to get in,' Hatch explained. 'Give it a go.'

I pulled the Slate from my pocket and waved it at the door.

'Welcome, Rees,' the computerised voice said, and the wooden door swung open with a satisfying creak.

Beyond the door lay a valley of enchanting greenery. I gazed up at a bright blue sky, clear save for the occasional puff of white cumulus. The grass was dry and smooth under my shoes, and half a dozen apple trees were casting protective shadows over beautiful wooden benches. I could feel the warmth of the sun on my skin. In the distance, a huge waterfall was roaring down a cliff edge. There were people in swimwear playing in a pool at its base.

It was like being back on the surface. But the rolling hills, as they spread out to the horizon, suddenly turned into a giant metal scaffold. Strange.

'As you can see, the Garden is not yet finished,' Hatch

said. 'They need more workers to get the job done.' He sat down on one of the benches. 'Nothing here is real, but if you sit right here and look out, it's the most beautiful garden you've ever visited.'

'Are those sheep over there?' I asked, pointing at a smattering of white spots on one of the distant hills.

'No,' he answered. 'They're clouds that haven't yet been lifted into the sky.'

I looked, smiling, at the vast blue stratosphere above. Who needed real sun and blue skies in a place like this? But there was something that wasn't right. Something was missing ...

'There's no birds singing,' I said.

'Birds have been a problem,' replied Hatch. 'They tend to hit their heads against the sky, or they fly into the sun and get burned.'

'How ... horrible.'

'Mechanical birds are being considered. But for now, there's a bird-sound machine if you want it.'

Hatch opened a latch on the tree behind him and pressed a button.

'Croak!' said the tree.

'Oh dear, it's set on raven,' Hatch said. He pressed another button, and the song of the nightingale washed down the valley. 'Lovely. Take a minute to walk around, Rees, and clear your head. But don't stray too far and fall off the horizon! Some silly buggers have already found themselves in the medical wing after not looking where they were going.'

I wandered down to the river that flowed through the valley from the waterfall. The water was full of coins from every country in the world. I lay on my belly, extending my arm into the cold, biting water, and grabbed a handful of the money. There were yen pieces there, American cents, pennies, pesetas, kwachas, some euros.

I wish Megan was here to see this with me, I thought with deep longing. The wet silver in my hand shone in the false sun above. But I knew it was silly to want to go home. Only last night I'd tried to run away, feeling thoroughly miserable about my life. I just wished I could have told Megan where I was going before I went. She'd only think I'd run away again.

I dropped the money back into the river, where it sank into the obscure darkness, out of sight. Standing up, I grabbed an apple from the branches of one of the nearby trees.

'Careful now!' Hatch shouted. 'The apples aren't edible yet!' His mouth went crooked as if he was reliving an unpleasant experience.

I strode up the hill and sat down next to him.

'Do you like it?' he asked.

'Yes. But I don't get it. How? How does this all exist?'

'The Garden?'

'No – Cantref Gwaelod. I just can't accept it.'

'That's the second big surprise of the day, and it's a less pleasant one, I'm afraid,' he said. 'Take out your Slate and point it at the sky.'

I did as he asked.

'Now, command your Slate to show you how we got here.'

'Slate,' I said, a little worried about what I'd discover. 'What is Cantref Gwaelod doing here?'

The sunlight in the Garden faded and the sky above took on the aspect of a black, moonless night. As my eyes adjusted, I realised I was looking up at millions of stars, more than I'd ever seen before. It was so clear that I could see the shape of the Milky Way in a wide band across the sky.

'This was the sky thousands of years ago,' Hatch said. 'Before cities. Before any kind of artificial light.'

'I've never seen it so bright.'

'You see there?' Hatch pointed up beyond the boughs of the trees. I saw a light speeding forward. A shooting star? It was blinking, like a satellite. No, there were two of them, one following the other.

The lights approached and came closer and took on a shape. Two spaceships, one much larger than the other. And the larger one was attacking the smaller one. Bolts of fire, like lasers or missiles, were peppering its rear. Fire and billowing smoke erupted from the smaller craft as it was knocked off course. It tumbled down, narrowly avoiding the efforts of the larger ship to finish it off.

'It's going to hit us!' I said, ducking under the bench just as the smaller spaceship, which must have been two miles across, swept over our heads.

'Don't worry,' Hatch said, 'it's just a projection.'

I heard a deep rumble behind us, presumably as the smaller ship hit the Earth.

'The Cantref wasn't a city – it was a space station,' Hatch said. 'It didn't drown. It crashed, some thirty miles off the shore of Cardigan Bay.'

Hatch raised his Slate and the stars disappeared. I blinked.

'But ... what about Seithenyn and the doors?' I asked.

'Well, there is some truth to that. One of the hangar gates wasn't closed. If it had been, we may have been able to float. And it was Seithenyn's fault. As it was, the ship sank like a rock to the bottom of the ocean.'

'So, what happened afterwards?'

'We got out. Of course, the people of Britain didn't know we were aliens. They thought we were gods, because our technology was so superior to theirs. They worshipped us, and built their own megaliths and tombs covered in our own star-maps. The stone circles at Cardiff centre, for example.' Hatch smiled. 'The Celts were not a primitive people, you see. Their culture, their art, was alien.'

I was gobsmacked. 'But ... why didn't you just fix the ship and fly home?'

'Some of our technology survived the crash but no one had the knowledge needed to fix the ship. Since then, we've been slowly rebuilding so that we can take off again one day, and travel back home. But most of our focus has been on defence.'

'Defence?' I leaned in. 'Against what?'

'That's a story for another day,' Hatch said. 'It can be a lot to take in.' He nudged me with his elbow. 'You should take the rest of the day off, my friend. Wander around. Relax.'

I stood up and saw spots in front of my eyes.

'Come to think of it, I am feeling a little light-headed.'

'It's the change in pressure,' Hatch said. 'I'll show you to your room.'

CHAPTER 6

THE ROOM-MATE

'Welcome, Rees,' a computerised voice said.

The door slid open and I stepped into my new home.

The room was dark, except for a pale blue light coming from one large window. A blind was closed half-way down to keep some of the light out.

'You have to aim your Slate at the lamp to turn it on,' said Hatch.

I took the device from my pocket and pointed it to the ceiling. The room became filled with bright light and I could suddenly make out a shape on the couch. A man lay there, his black hair like two long cascades of oil covering his face.

'You awake, Brân?' Hatch asked.

No answer came, only the sound of quiet snoring.

'Your room-mate must have had a busy day.'

'Room-mate?' I asked.

Hatch nodded. 'It's a communal apartment. We feel that human contact is good for people.'

'That's fine by me,' I said, thinking about the hostel. 'I'm used to it.'

I looked around the room. It reminded me of a luxury

apartment in a glossy magazine. Apart from the couch, there was a table, a rug on the floor, and a cupboard topped with a flower vase. There were four doors and two of those were open, one leading to a kitchen and the other to a bedroom. The only unusual thing about the room was that it had an amazing view of the sea bed.

I noticed the young man on the couch lifting his head and brushing the hair from his face. He stared at me, blinking.

'Who are you?'

'I've brought your new housemate,' said Hatch. 'Brân, this is Rees.'

'Hi,' I said, uncertainly.

Brân peeped at me from between his black curtains of hair. He had a thin, grey face, which seemed greyer still in contrast to his bright orange shirt.

'Uh, hi,' he said sleepily.

'Well, that's it, I'll let you get to know each other,' said Hatch, clapping his hands together. 'Brân will be able to help you with anything you need, Rees. But give me a shout on your Slate if anything big is bothering you.'

He went out the door and slipped back into the crowd. The door closed behind him and the noise of the corridor faded with it.

Brân was staring at me, anxiously.

'What are you wearing?' he asked at last.

I shrugged. 'Normal clothes.'

'They're not normal here. You'd better change your shirt. There's a handful of them in the bedroom. You're in the room on the left.'

I went through to my room and took it all in. I hadn't had my own space in years. There was a bed, a table, and a drawer. A door to the side of the room led to a narrow bathroom. It was bare, but I suppose that my job was to fill it. With possessions, life, memories. I felt like I'd just won the lottery.

I opened a drawer and found it was full of identical black trousers and light blue shirts. I changed and went back to the living room.

'Design and Upkeep,' Brân said.

'What?'

'Blue shirt. You'll be in the Design and Upkeep Department.'

'Doing what?'

He shrugged. 'Whatever they do there. Designing spaceships, buildings and so on, and maintaining them ...'

I made a face. 'I don't know how to do any of those things.'

'They can inject the skill into your head. It's the ideas they're after. The creative part is what computers can't crack.'

'But I've never been able to get a proper job.' My mouth was dry. 'I was homeless before Hatch came for me.'

'So was I! They do tend to go for the people who are ... unconnected.'

'You were homeless?'

'I grew up of the streets of Swansea, poor as a church mouse, making a living selling bits of coal that fell off the wagon ways down to the docks.' He grinned proudly, showing teeth that were bright white but wonky. 'That feels like a long time ago now, though. But I suppose you never stop being thankful for the opportunity you've been given.'

I curled my lip. 'I've never seen any coal wagons in Swansea. How long have you been here?'

'I don't exactly remember. Time works differently at Cantref Gwaelod. There is no day and night, the weeks and months dovetail ...' He grimaced. 'It was a very, very long time ago. About a century and a half?'

I gaped at him. 'A century and a half?'

'Yes. They'll keep you going here, if you're useful to them. You'll occasionally need a new kidney or something.'

I got up and stared out of the window. The other buildings glowed like crystals in the darkness. Would I go mad, staying in the same place for centuries?

'How have they kept this place hidden for so long?' I asked.

Brân shrugged. 'Nothing down here but a few jellyfish. It's easier to get to the moon than the bottom of the sea.' He smiled again. 'Listen, you'll get used to it. Everyone here has. It's normal to feel homesick at first.'

Homesick, I thought. Perhaps that was why I was so agitated. I'd never had a proper home to be sick about before. What I'd considered home was *the surface of the Earth*, and now I'd left it.

'So, what section are you in?' I asked, looking at his bright orange shirt.

Brân fiddled with the button on his sleeve. 'I'm not supposed to say.'

'Why not?'

'It's a secret.'

'Well, you can tell me. I don't know anyone else, so I won't gossip.'

His eyes darted around the room. 'Let me show you where my room is,' he said a little bit too loudly and robotically, as if he wasn't talking to me at all.

I frowned. 'Your room?' I could see where his room was from where I was sat.

He jumped up from the sofa and beckoned me to follow him through the door. His bedroom was, as I'd suspected, identical to mine. But he walked on into the bathroom, gesturing with his finger for me to follow, and closed the door. Then he turned on the shower at full blast.

I stepped back, embarrassed, half expecting him to start undressing.

'Right, they don't keep an eye on us in here,' he whispered. 'And they shouldn't be able to hear us, either.'

'Who are they?'

'I'll tell you where I work because they won't, until it's too late for you to change your mind. But don't say I told you!' He pointed an accusing finger.

'I won't!'

He moved so close that I could feel his black hair tickling my ear. My nose was filled with a pungent, pickle-like odour.

'I'm in the Elimination Department,' he said, quietly.

'What's the Elimination Department?'

'We eliminate people,' he whispered, stepping back.

'Why is that a secret?'

'Because they told you that you can go home.'

I stared at him. 'But I can go home, if I want,' I said aloud. 'Hatch said. He told me —'

Brân put a finger over his lips, then drew it across his neck. 'Not after they've wiped you out,' he said quietly.

'What do you mean, wiped me out?'

'Killed you.'

'Killed me?' I yelled.

'Shh. Not down here. Up there. In the real world. They don't want people to know what's going on down here.

51

So, they're going to make everyone think you're dead.'

I balked. 'But how?'

'That's my job. Well, me and the rest of the Elimination Department.' Brân eyed the room suspiciously, his eyes settling on our reflection in the mirror, as if he suspected us of listening in to our own conversation.

'Sometimes families accept that people have disappeared,' he continued. 'But sometimes they ask questions, start researching it, meet other people who've lost loved ones. So, we have to convince them that you're gone forever.'

'How?'

'I'll show you, once you've decided to stay,' he said. 'Once you've made that choice, they'll let you know about the Elimination Department. But I'm not supposed to tell you anything yet.'

He shut off the shower and I followed him out of the steam-filled bathroom and back into the living room.

I sat heavily on the couch. I didn't know what to think by now. Had I done the right thing, leaving Megan? Was I already dead? I didn't want to be 'erased' from her life. I'd thought I could visit her ... during the holidays – did they even have holidays here?

I felt as if the whole weight of the sea above was pressing down on me.

'Are you all right?' Brân asked. 'You look a little pale.'

'I'm getting a headache.'

'Don't worry about that. Your body has to get used to being so far below the sea. You're sure to feel a little off at first.' He nodded, thoughtfully. 'I'm sorry if I scared you. It's easy to forget how strange this city is to new arrivals.'

I took a deep breath. 'I'm going to have a lie down,' I said. Hopefully, things would look a little clearer in the morning. If there was such a thing as morning, down here.

CHAPTER 7

THE DREAM

I dreamt that I was standing on a wide, empty desert, full of little yellow stones. The sky was a metallic silver and a green mist hung over the land. At the far end of the plain I could see what looked like a small village with huts built from the mud of the surrounding soil. It looked alien but felt like home.

I could see creatures. Not human – they were too bony and tall – but I knew that they had built the village. They looked like nothing I'd ever seen before, but I knew I was one of them. Suddenly they were moving – all of them running towards me, mad with fear. I could feel it. I shared it.

Then a pulse of air hit me and the village exploded in blue and purple flames. The creatures were overtaken by the blasted earth and fire and thrown in the air. Everything important to me was consumed right there and then.

I fell to the ground in despair. I'd lost so much, my entire family. I lay there, dust and ash sticking to my tear-soaked face. And I had a very strong feeling: that the only thing to ease my pain would be hatred and revenge.

I woke up. My headache was completely gone. Perhaps Brân was right – that after time the body got used to living at the bottom of the sea. But what a strange dream. It had felt so real, as if it had really happened. And I was still left with the feelings of grief, pain and a desire for revenge.

Then I noticed the girl in the room.

'Hello, Rees,' she said.

I must have jumped a whole two feet out of bed. I grabbed the blanket and pulled it up to my chest. She was squatting in the corner. She was beautiful, with lovely green eyes. Despite the light being dim, she seemed to glitter all over, as if made of light. What the hell was she doing in my room, in the middle of the night, without my permission? But then I remembered: there was no day and night here. I'd turned off the light, that was all.

'Who ... who are you?' I asked.

'Awen,' she replied. 'We've met before, don't you remember?'

I'd never seen her before, but there was something familiar about her voice. Then it clicked. She was the silvery green doe who had called to me in the park. My stomach turned as I remembered that journey through the forest, to the edge of the lake, where I'd seen my family in the water ...

'You were an animal the last time we met,' I pointed out. 'I thought it was a dream or ... something.'

Awen leapt up from where she was sitting and bounced across the bed. There was still something animal-like about her – a lean and hungry look on her face, unkempt hair.

'You have to help me, Rees.' She pushed her face in towards mine just as she had her snout in the park. 'Do you remember the dream you just had?'

'What? In the forest? But —'

'No. The one you had just now?'

I drew myself back against the headboard. 'How do you know I've just had a dream?'

'I showed you that dream. I thought it only fair you get a peek inside my mind, since I got a peek inside yours at the park. It seems we have quite a bit in common. Painful memories.' Her eyes flicked around the room as if she was readying herself to flee at any second. 'That was my family you saw destroyed. You were watching through my eyes. You know what it's like to lose your family, don't you?'

I shuddered and tried to push the memory back down, deep, deep down under the blackest water of my mind.

'You feel guilty,' she said, 'about what happened.'

I nodded.

'I do too,' Awen said. 'I wasn't able to save my family that day. That's why I need you to help me. I want revenge, Rees.'

I heard a noise coming from the living room beyond the door. Brân.

'There's no point talking to your new friend about me,' Awen said. 'He won't be able to see me. I only exist in your mind. Everyone will think you're crazy.'

'Brân!' I jumped out of bed, scooting past the ghostly woman, and went out through the door to the living room. Brân was lying on the couch, his head propped up and hair hanging down over his Slate.

'You alright, Rees?' he asked. 'How you feeling now?'

'I'm, um, OK ...'

Then I noticed Awen standing in the far corner of the room. I jumped. I hadn't seen her go past. Brân didn't seem to notice her at all. I looked from one to the other as if they were playing a round of tennis.

'Can I ask a question?' I asked. 'Is it normal ... to see things ... here?'

'Like what?'

'Like people ... that no one else can see?'

Brân shook his head. 'You look very pale, Rees. Maybe you should go back to bed if you don't feel well. Just record on your Slate that you're sick and they won't expect you to go in to work.'

'No, I'm fine,' I squeaked. 'I reckon a short walk will help clear my mind. Where do we get breakfast around here?'

'I'll show you now in a minute.'

'OK, I'll change first.'

I went to the bathroom and threw cold water over my face. I brushed my teeth, filled a glass from the tap, then drank it, letting the water slowly flow between my dry lips.

'Are you ignoring me?' Awen had appeared in the bathroom mirror behind me.

I dropped the glass and it smashed across the white tiles.

'A little privacy would be nice!'

'I'm inside your mind,' said Awen. 'I've seen everything there is to see.'

'It's the outside things I'm most concerned about.' I turned to face her. 'What are you then? Another microchip that's been planted in my brain?'

'No. If you listen, I'll explain. I'm a creature from another planet. The one I showed you in the dream.'

'But how are you inside my head?'

'That's what people from my planet do. We live inside other things.'

'Like a parasite?'

She made a face. 'That's a very negative way of putting it. Think of me as a room-mate, like Brân there. You're used to sharing space with others, you said so yourself.'

'I'm used to sharing a bedroom, not my head!'

'Think of it as teamwork. I want revenge on those who killed my family, you see, and you're going to help me do that.'

'That's not teamwork, that's me doing what you want. Why would I? I do things I want to do.'

'Because you're my hero.' She flashed a gap-toothed smile.

I blushed. She was incredibly beautiful, and her voice was like silk. Then I remembered she could read my mind and blushed even more.

'Would you mind leaving the room as I change?' I asked.

'Of course. Provided you *do* help me.' And with that, she disappeared.

My new clothes were rumpled and sweaty from tossing and turning in bed. I peeled them off as if they were old skin. Then I cleared the glass fragments from the bathroom floor and had a quick shower.

Even though the girl was gone, her voice continued to babble on in my mind. She talked about her own planet, how the monsters from space had destroyed it, and that the monsters were on their way to Earth to destroy her, and I was her only hope of defeating them.

'Monsters?' I asked, rubbing some strange blue paste which I hoped was shampoo into my hair.

'Yes, like dragons, you'd call them. Giant lizards, their

mouths full of teeth, and they have huge wings.'

'Hold on. You've got the wrong boy if you think I'm going to fight dragons.'

'If you follow my instructions it will be easy-peasy.'

I sighed. 'Listen, Awen. I've seen so many weird things over the last 24 hours, I'm not sure what to believe anymore. I can just about accept a city at the bottom of the sea, flying saucers, Welsh speakers running the world, and who knows what else.' I put my head under the faucet and let out a sigh of relief when the blue paste came out in big dollops of foam.

'Perhaps you exist,' I said, 'but it's more likely that I'm a little bit stressed, or I've got an infection, or something. I'm going to make an appointment with the doctor. If they have doctors here. But until then, I'm going to ignore you, OK?' I held my hands out under the shower then rubbed the water in my eyes to get the soap out of them. 'If you really do exist, you're welcome to jump into someone else's head, and I think that would be best, because there is not a snowball's chance in hell that I'm going to be fighting dragons from space. OK?'

I heard Brân's voice from the next room. 'Are you OK, Rees? Who are you talking to?'

'Just calling someone on my Slate,' I replied. 'I'll be out now.' I dried myself, got dressed and walked out into the living room.

'You're going to love the canteen,' said Brân, grabbing his jacket.

'I know you're afraid,' said Awen. 'But you can't keep running forever.'

'Shh,' I said ...

'What?' asked Brân, stopping at the door.

'Sorry, it's just the noisy air con,' I said.

I can live with this, I thought, following Brân out of the room. A voice inside your head isn't such a bad thing. Apparently, all the famous mathematicians and artists had them. Two heads are better than one, that's what everyone says.

'Rees,' Awen said.

'What do you want now?' I whispered, my hand over my mouth.

'You follow Brân to the canteen. You won't be any use to me starving,' said Awen. 'Let's talk further over a meal.'

They're wrong, I thought. Two heads are not better than one. Two heads are bloody annoying.

'Oi,' said Awen. 'I heard that.'

CHAPTER 8

HERE BE DRAGONS

'You can ask for anything you want,' Brân said.

'Anything?'

'Well, anything edible. A ham sandwich, chocolate ice cream, soup, chips, fish fingers ... or something more adventurous. You can order a tub of caviar in a crocodile's foot if you like.'

The canteen was a large, rectangular room, with rows and rows of tables in a long line, enough to seat over five hundred people. There were large screens on the walls with rolling news about new developments at Cantref Gwaelod, including cybernetic limbs that would allow workers to lift ten times their own body weight, and a new Slate that would let you download books straight into your brain.

The leader of Cantref Gwaelod, Gwyddno Garanhir, seemed to feature in almost every report. He looked just like his statue, with a craggy face behind a grey-streaked beard and large bushy eyebrows. But a little fatter. Perhaps he had got older, or maybe the sculptor had flattered him.

The clock said it was just before 7am, and the canteen

wasn't crowded so early in the morning, but there was already a queue to fetch food. The people behind me were getting impatient because I was taking so long to make my mind up. It was harder to choose when you could choose ... well, *anything*.

'But where does it get the food from?' I asked, unable to grasp the fact that caviar in a crocodile's foot could be inside such a small machine.

Brân shrugged. 'It just prints it.'

'Prints food?' I stared at the machine, queasy. I decided to play it safe and chose exactly what I had every day at the shelter. 'Sausage, beans and chips, please.' I aimed my Slate at the device. The machine produced a bowl and spat the meal out into it.

'You can have anything, and you order *that*?' Brân asked in disbelief.

'Comfort food. I need it at the moment.'

Brân ordered a full breakfast, with several pieces of bacon, beans, egg, black pudding, waffles, and brown sauce.

'You have to learn to be more ambitious!' he told me as I gazed enviously at the mountain of food on his plate.

'All of that will give you a heart attack,' I said.

'I'll just ask for a new heart.'

I had a look around for somewhere to sit. And then I saw Hatch, sitting alone at the far end, and walked over to greet him. At least he knew me.

'Is it OK for us to sit here?'

Hatch looked up from his food. He was munching on some green mash and yellow beans.

'Yes, and welcome,' he replied, with a friendly smile. 'I won't whisk you off to any strange environs this time, Rees. Are you settling in?'

'Yes, I think. I've had some headaches.'

'There are plenty of doctors available if you want to see one. They'll fight over you; almost no one gets sick at Cantref Gwaelod.'

'I don't want to be too late for work,' I said, jabbing at my food.

'Oh, there's no need to work set hours,' Hatch said. 'Once you feel like you've finished what needs to be done and you've done your very best, go for a restaurant supper, go to the library, watch some sports.'

As Hatch spoke, Awen appeared on the seat beside him. She smiled, the gap between her front teeth seeming even larger than before. I tried to ignore her and think about something else to talk about.

'I can prove to you that I'm not a figment of your imagination,' she said, her fingers scuttling across the table towards me. 'In just a few seconds an alarm will go off. The dragons are coming to get me.'

Brân sat back and belched.

'There's no need to stuff your mouth, Brân,' said Hatch, disapprovingly.

'A full belly will always have your back, that's what my grandmother used to say!' replied Brân. 'Starving on the back streets of terraced houses has taught me never to refuse any food that's offered to me.'

'Yes, but I'm not sure you count as a growing boy any more,' Hatch said, his high cheekbones jutting as he smiled.

'So I'll stop ageing too?' I asked.

'Once you've decided to stay,' replied Hatch, pointing his fork at me. 'Then we can stop your cells from degenerating further. But the decision is permanent – once you've made it, you can never go back.'

I looked at my hands. It was strange to think that this would be my body forever. OK, I'd never have to get old. But growing up was a part of life, in a way. A part of life I'd never experience if I stayed here.

'So what happens if I don't decide to stay?'

Hatch shifted uncomfortably in his seat. 'You know, it's never come up.'

I didn't like that answer. 'But what if I don't want to?'

Suddenly a loud alarm rang out above us and the room flashed red.

Hatch and Brân looked at each other in surprise.

'Practice alarm?' Brân asked.

'I didn't know about it,' Hatch said. He stood up. 'OK, everyone back to work! You know the drill.'

He ran from the canteen and down the corridor, leaving his food half-eaten.

'Go back to the Garden and wait there,' Brân said.

'What does the alarm mean?' I asked.

He made a face, shrugging. 'It means Cantref Gwaelod is under threat. Probably ... probably a false alarm.' He got up and left the room, which was rapidly emptying as a great throng of people hurried for the exit.

Awen looked at me, pursing her lips smugly. 'Is that proof enough for you?'

'How did you —?'

'I knew the dragons were coming,' she said. 'I just arrived two days before them. They're after me, remember?'

'You've brought them here?'

'Don't worry, this is all part of the plan. You are part of the plan. Together we're going to save the Earth, and you're going to get the credit. I did say you were destined for something greater.'

The large screens on the canteen walls had stopped showing the news and now Gwyddno Garanhir appeared, staring solemnly into the camera.

'People of Cantref Gwaelod, hear me now,' he said in a clear, resounding politician's voice. 'Earlier this morning we received a message from the Space Observation Department saying that they had recorded the entry of an unidentified object into our solar system. It has just passed Jupiter and is on a direct collision course with Earth. However, this is not an asteroid. It is what we believe to be the ship of an enemy combatant.' His bushy eyebrows rose like ships taking off. 'Indeed, we believe that it belongs to the same race of aliens that shot us down over Earth, thousands of years ago ...'

The image suddenly became blurry and pixelated, as if the screen had lost its wireless signal.

And now a different face appeared on the screen – if you could call it a face. It had scaly, red skin, giant teeth, a wide forehead and huge horns growing out of its temples.

I felt Awen's anger shaking through every bone in my body.

'It's him!' she said. 'The one who killed my family.'

'Creatures of Earth,' said the dragon, huskily. 'I will only say this once, so pay attention.'

It was clear that some translation tool was in place, as the dragon's mouth was not quite moving with the words.

'I am Drachfolga Bolorembus, Emperor of Dragons. Know that we could destroy your planet with the touch of a button if we so wished.' It blew smoke and sparks from its huge nostrils. 'Two days ago, a terrorist agent landed on your planet. She is a great threat to us and has already caused massive destruction to our ships across the galaxy. You must hand her over within 12 hours or we will be forced to destroy your entire planet to ensure she does not escape.'

The dragon's face disappeared from the screen and it became pixelated once more. Gwyddno Garanhir's face reappeared, his forehead shining with sweat.

'Can I talk to him?' he asked. 'Is he gone?' He then looked straight into the camera. 'All air crew to hangar one. Everyone else, back to work.' The screen went blank.

Awen leaned over the table. 'Now I'm going to tell you what I need you to do.'

CHAPTER 9

IN THE WEEDS

'You want me to do what?'

'Steal a spaceship and fly up to the dragon's ship,' Awen said. 'And then disable it.'

'I can't do that!'

'You don't have to do anything apart from listen to me. Everything will be fine!'

'Listen, Awen. I've told you. I'm not a hero! You've got the wrong person. Jump into someone else's ear.'

'It's your destiny,' she said. 'Don't be so pathetic.'

I glared at her. At this point in an argument I'd usually walk away in a huff, but that was pointless in this case.

'I just don't like other people depending on me,' I said. 'I'm bad at it! I can look after myself, but I don't like getting things wrong and hurting other people.'

I got up, scraping back my chair, and left. The corridor was in complete bedlam. Everyone was rushing around with panicked faces and the alarm continued to sound. The entire sea floor had turned blood-red as every emergency light in Cantref Gwaelod flashed.

'Where are you going?' Awen asked.

'To work – that's what they've asked me to do.'

'We don't have time for that!'

'If you don't have time for it, then get out of my head!' I knocked the side of my face with my palm, as if it would dislodge her through my ear.

I turned left towards the Garden. I pulled my Slate from my pocket and waved it at the door.

'Welcome, Rees,' the door said.

The Garden was an oasis of calm in the middle of a raging storm. The heavy oak door creaked closed behind me and I couldn't hear the alarm at all, just the gushing of the waterfall. I took a deep, calming breath and looked around. The thought of working here, of shaping the landscape, creating beautiful forests, filled me with joy. It was paradise.

'I don't care what you do,' I said. 'I'm staying here. They chose me for a reason, out of everyone.'

'They chose you because you were homeless and could disappear easily.'

I paused. 'Just shut up.'

I spotted another blue-shirted worker on his hands and knees tending to a row of flowers. He had a ginger goatee and a shaved bald head. His Slate was propped up next to him so that he could watch the news about the dragon ship.

'Excuse me,' I said.

He looked up and brushed the loose grass off his knees.

'Hi. I'm working here, I think,' I said.

'Oh great,' he said. 'We're a small team but we do important work. It's nice to meet you!'

He took off a pair of green gardening gloves and shook my hand.

'It's about time we got a new weeder.'

I stared at him. 'A new what?'

'Weeder. The place has been growing wild since the last guy left us. It's getting serious, mate. First, you'll need to do these here, and then there's a load more down by the waterfall.'

'Weeding? And what do I do once I've finished doing that?'

He laughed, heartily. 'Well, the Garden is a thousand acres. By the time you're done at one end they will have grown back on the other. It is eternal summer here after all.'

My eyes bulged. 'Weeding – forever? You guys brought me here ... I left everything, because you want me to ... weed?'

He seemed taken aback. 'Cantref Gwaelod is like all other cities. Who do you think collects your rubbish, cleans your shirts?' He crossed his arms. 'Not every job can be a glamorous one, mate.'

'Don't they have robots to do this stuff?'

He scratched his head with his gloveless hand. 'I

suppose it's quite a complex job, teaching a robot to be able to differentiate between a plant you don't want and one you do. And the people who *could* do that have more important things to worry about, I'm afraid, especially when there's so much surplus labour on the surface.'

I looked around in despair. Now that I was aware of them, I could see weeds *everywhere*. Enough to keep me occupied forever, really.

I stooped down to pull one of them, roots and all, from the soil. 'But you say the guy who used to do this job left?' I asked hopefully.

'No, he *left* us. He died.'

'I thought no one died here.'

'Oh, people do. Those that want to go. They just stop going to the regeneration chambers.' He laughed again, thumping me on the back. 'I suppose he just got bored with the weeding!'

I looked at the shrivelled up weed in my hand. Unwanted. Uprooted.

I am a weed, I thought.

Awen appeared nearby, sitting on one of the benches. She pushed her hand through her hair.

'Going well?' she asked.

I flung the weed away and sat next to her, staring vacantly into space.

'You know, I really thought for a minute that I was

going to get to be someone,' I said. I laughed, but it came out hollow-sounding. 'Doing something I wanted to do, you know? That they'd discovered some kind of inner talent I had that I wasn't aware of.' I looked down at my muddy palms. 'But I suppose I'm just a loser, like I always thought.'

Awen sighed. 'Look, Rees. No one on Earth, or in the rest of the galaxy, for that matter, is just naturally good at anything. People become good at things by being taught to be good at them.' She gave me a stern look. 'You're no good at anything because the second someone tries to get close to you – teachers, lovers, aliens from distant worlds – you push them away.'

'Just leave me alone!' I snapped. The other gardener looked over in confusion.

'You're just proving my point,' Awen said.

I marched to the pool at the bottom of the waterfall. It was empty of people now. I could see my own reflection playing on the surface, but the bottom was too deep to see.

'You have to let it go,' Awen said, her voice gentle as the breeze. 'You made one mistake, one easy mistake.'

'Why can't you leave me alone?'

'Your dad was driving. He should have driven more carefully.'

I looked down into the depths and saw their faces

looking up at me. My mother, sister and father. My mother's mouth moving soundlessly.

'*Come home, Rees.*'

'It's OK,' Awen said. I felt her hand on my shoulder. How could I feel her hand if she wasn't really there?

'I just want to be alone, like I said.'

'Want and need are different things,' Awen said. 'You've wanted to be alone your whole life and it's solved nothing. What you need is to learn to let people in, to rely on them, and let them rely on you. And you need to let people tell you it's not your fault. People like me.'

I turned and stared into her pale green eyes. There was something magical about them. A warmth that I wanted in my life. No, that I *needed*.

'Can I trust you?' I asked.

'It's up to you,' she said. 'We've both lost everything. And we both blame ourselves. But we can also make up for it. Together, we can make up for it.' She reached over and held out her hand. 'So, do you want to do that, or stay here weeding?'

I took her hand and squeezed it.

CHAPTER 10

THE SLATE

'The first thing you need to do is steal someone else's Slate,' Awen said.

'Why?'

'You can't leave Cantref Gwaelod using yours. You'll need to steal one from someone who's been here for a long time and has access to the outside.'

I walked along one of the long corridors, following Awen's instructions. It was as crowded as a New York sidewalk and people bumped against me as they jostled past. The alarm had now stopped but the red lights were still flashing, and it was clear that the crisis was not over.

'But I don't know anyone. How am I supposed to know how long someone's been here?'

'You know one person. You can stop here.'

I looked up at the sign on the door. 'The Elimination Department? I'm not going to steal from Brân.'

'Brân won't be any the wiser,' Awen said. 'People lose their Slates all the time. He can just order a new one.'

I pointed my Slate at the door, but it didn't open. 'No access,' I said with relief.

'You'll have to wait until someone else opens the door,

and then gain entry.'

I stayed there for a good five minutes, rocking on my heels, the only person standing in the middle of the buzzing crowd.

Suddenly the door flew open and a heavy-set man hurried out, colliding with my shoulder.

'Oops, sorry,' he said, before disappearing into the crowd.

I slipped in through the door before it closed again.

I was in an open plan office of some sort. But in reality there were several rooms, each separated by a glass wall. Urgent meetings were taking place at oval tables and several people sat at large touchscreens.

I immediately saw a problem.

'Everyone here is wearing a yellow shirt and I'm wearing a blue shirt!' I whispered. 'They'll notice me right away.'

'They'll notice you even sooner if you keep talking to yourself.'

'For God's sake, Awen —'

'Don't worry, all you have to do is find Brân before you're seen.'

This is the stupidest plan ever! I thought.

'Hey,' said Awen. 'Don't call me stupid.'

Groaning, I walked with as much authority as I could through the glass maze. Everyone was so busy that I seemed to escape their notice. I guessed there were at least two hundred people in the office, but I couldn't see Brân anywhere. It didn't help that everyone was wearing exactly the same thing.

'Look – there are stairs over there,' Awen said. 'Perhaps Brân is on another floor.'

'I hate this.' I was about to walk down the stairs when another man came up to meet me, carrying a pile of multicoloured tubes. He saw me and stopped.

'The Design and Upkeep Department, isn't it? The bodies are down a floor to the left if you want to sign them off. What happened to Edwina?'

'She's, um, ill.'

He raised his eyebrows. 'She hasn't missed a day for half a century or more. Well, we have to keep going, especially on a day like this.'

He pushed past me and hurried off, shaking his head. I had a quick look either way and descended the stairs.

I soon realised that I was below seabed level, deeper still into the rock. My ears popped as I went down. The stairway led to a corridor shabbier than any part of Cantref Gwaelod I'd seen so far. The light was low and I could hear a dripping noise. This part of the city seemed to have been built much earlier than the rest.

There were doors on either side of the corridor, a long row of them, with regular handles rather than mechanical ones. I chose the first one on the left and stepped into another dark room. There was a strange smell of decaying meat. I pointed my Slate at the light.

'No, don't!' Awen said. 'If you use your Slate, they'll be on to you.'

I stuffed it back in my pocket and wiped the sweat off my brow. I felt along the wall. If there were handles on the doors there might be a light switch.

'This one will be shipped out to Australia tomorrow,' I heard a voice say by the door.

I slid to the far end of the room and crouched behind what seemed to be a table. The door opened and two people stood there – Brân and a blonde woman.

'The Canadian girl will need to be moved up soon too,' said the woman. 'Roger just needs to double-check how she died. I think we're going for falling into a frozen lake.'

Brân was diligently taking notes on his Slate. 'OK, Edwina. I'll need a few more hours to finish with the boy from Afghanistan.'

'What's left to finish?'

'I need to model the legs and one of the hands.'

'Well, we're saying he was blown up by a drone. Surely we could leave off a few body parts ...'

Brân waved his Slate absent-mindedly to turn on the light and I quickly lay down on my belly. I looked up. The long room was full of tables and someone ...

or something ... was lying on each one.

'They look fine to me,' Edwina said. 'I want them out within the hour. Who knows how busy things will be from now on. We might need hundreds of new employees to deal with these flaming lizards. I mean, maybe we could pretend that the dragons have eaten them all ...?'

The door was closed again but the light stayed on.

I slid back along the wall, making sure not to touch the bodies on the tables. They weren't real bodies, I thought, just incredibly realistic fakes created to make people think their owners were really dead, but ...

But what if they *weren't* fake?

Distracted, I bumped into something – a foot. I recoiled as if a spider had fallen on my shoulder. The foot, in a white Reebok, was sticking out from under the sheet and it —

Holy shit, I whispered, edging closer to examine the shoe. It was mine. I could swear it. Down to the star-shaped biro doodle on the side of the white leather that I'd once done, bored, while waiting to be seen by a Universal Credit agent.

I couldn't resist. I pulled back the sheet and looked down at my own decaying corpse.

'Oh my God!' I said aloud.

I didn't look good. My skin was bruised and swollen and covered in small cuts.

'Rees! What the hell —?'

I turned and saw Brân at the door. He looked even paler than usual.

'I ... came to see you ...'

'But how did you get into this section? You don't have the right.' He hurriedly closed the door behind him. 'We'll both be in big trouble if you're found here. New recruits aren't supposed to know about the Elimination Department in case you ...' He looked down at my body. 'Well, yes, that.'

'Me ... that's me!'

'Of course. I'm preparing your body to be transported to the surface.' He looked back and forth between us. 'I think it's quite a good likeness.'

I gazed down into my own empty, lifeless eyes. Like doll's eyes. 'I feel ... strangely violated. Don't you feel ... depressed, working among all these bodies?'

'Not at all. Bodies were commonplace when I was growing up. I survived the 1866 cholera epidemic, you know.' He pulled his Slate from his pocket. 'I remember the first body I saw ... my mother's body. When Hatch came to get me, I thought he was an angel.' He turned to face me. 'You can have a new heart, but the feelings never leave you.'

'What's happened to my ear?' I said.

'Chewed by a fox. I like to add small details like that to make it more realistic.' There was a hint of pride in his voice. 'You've been out in the woods for a while.'

'But how did I die?'

'Who cares? You were homeless. Your kind turn up dead all the time.'

I felt as if I'd been punched in the gut. That was all I had amounted to in my life, I thought. A fox-chewed body that no one would care about.

'You can be someone,' Awen reminded me. 'You can save the Earth. But you need his Slate.'

I nodded. 'Brân, listen. I need to borrow your Slate. I need to flee Cantref Gwaelod and get back to the surface.'

'You can't, Rees.' He scraped his hands through his slick black hair, exasperated. 'It's too late. Cantref Gwaelod will never allow anyone to return to their lives on the surface. It's too dangerous. The risk involved —'

'But Hatch told me I don't have to stay here,' I said, shaking my head.

'You don't. You can leave at any time.' He smiled nervously. 'They'll just pop you out through the airlock.'

A shudder went through me. 'Are you serious?'

'Deadly serious.'

I turned away from him. I felt as if I couldn't breathe. As if I was trapped. Then I spun back. 'Why didn't you tell me?'

'Everyone stays!' Brân hissed, trying to keep his voice

down. 'Almost everyone. We do important work here. We can't let just anyone put it at risk.'

'Just anyone!' I pointed to the body on the table. 'Yeah, no one cares about people like me. That's what you said.' A speck of spit flew from my mouth.

He raised his hands in front of him. 'That's not what I meant, Rees. I was homeless too! Listen, you matter to us. You matter to me. I like you. And you were chosen, Rees, out of everyone.'

'To be a weeder!' I could feel tears sliding down my cheeks. I kicked one of the tables. 'I'm not even anyone. I'm no one.'

Then I looked into Brân's eyes and saw fear there, and I felt bad.

'I'm sorry, Brân. Listen,' I gabbled, approaching him. 'I know this sounds totally bonkers, but I have a voice in my head. An alien voice. And she says that only I can destroy the dragon spaceship.'

Brân took a step back. 'I don't think you're a hundred percent, Rees.' He took his Slate out of his pocket. 'But everything is going to be OK. I'm going to call you a doctor. You just stay here.'

I could feel myself losing control. I raised my hands and clenched my fists. I grabbed Brân by the neck and in one swift movement, cracked his head against the side of the nearest table. He fell to the floor, unconscious.

'Well done, Rees,' Awen said. 'You did what was necessary.'

'That wasn't me!' I protested. 'You ... took control of me.'

'I didn't do anything. Listen, the fate of the Earth is at stake. We have no time to waste discussing with —'

'You did that!'

'We've been through this, Rees. You can't just blame everyone else. Move on.'

'I don't want to help any more,' I said through gritted teeth, 'if you're just going to force me to hit my friends. What if I stayed here?'

'Here? Good luck. You've just attacked a colleague.'

I hesitated. 'You did that.'

'No one would believe you. Brân, your so-called friend, didn't believe you.'

Sweat was trickling down the nape of my neck. 'That's not fair.'

'I'll guide you, Rees. You'll be a hero. You will have saved the Earth. But you need to trust me.'

I felt defeated. 'OK, I'll do what you say, for now.' I leant down and fished Brân's Slate from the floor. 'But once this is over, everyone's going to know the truth.'

'Very good. Off we go. If you're going to get upset like this every time you have to hit someone today, it's going to be a long day.'

CHAPTER 11

INTO SPACE

The submarine hangar reminded me of the time, as a child, when I'd taken hold of a stick and started prodding an ants' nest. Chaos and mayhem. But then I'd looked closer and seen how all the little creatures seemed to know what their job was and where they were going.

Every few seconds the airlocks opened with a sucking noise as another fleet of *chwyrligwgan* shot out over the top of the hangar and out into the sea beyond. The larger ships were also being made ready for launch, their outer hulls stripped away as their decks were filled with cargo by three-storey cranes.

'Right,' said Awen. 'We need to come up with a plan.'

'I thought you had that all sorted out already.'

'Listen, if I could jump out of your head and walk on my own two legs, I would. But we need to steal a ship. There are so many leaving every minute, it shouldn't be too difficult. You should be able to just take one.'

I tried to appear as composed as possible. What was the worst thing that could happen? I strode towards the nearest ship and waved Brân's Slate at it, and its front door slid open. I ducked in and, after a quick look over

84

my shoulder to make sure no one had noticed me, I slid into position.

'That was easy,' said Awen.

'Well, you get very used to not being noticed when you're homeless,' I said, smiling wryly. 'Now, how do I fly this thing?'

I pulled the straps across my chest and prodded the ceiling. Menus filled with symbols appeared but were as nonsensical to me as Egyptian hieroglyphics.

'I can't make heads or tails of this.'

'Just try pressing something,' Awen suggested.

I gave one of the symbols a prod and felt the craft shudder.

'Here we go,' I said. 'Something's happening.'

But the *chwyrligwgan* just started spinning. And spinning some more. Not very quickly, but enough to make me feel sick as the hangar beyond the see-through walls rotated around me.

I heard the rap of knuckles on the craft.

'Hello? Is there someone in there?' a man asked.

'What do I do?' I said, sweating through my shirt. For once, Awen was quiet. 'You've abandoned me now, have you?'

'I'm thinking.'

'Think harder. You're the brains of this operation.'

'I'm in *your* brain. And to be honest I don't have much

to work with.'

'Oh, shut up,' I said, pressing another button, and the ship finally stopped spinning. Just as I was about to let out a heavy sigh of relief, it began hopping up and down like a rabbit.

A large crowd had now gathered around, entranced by the ship's actions.

'This isn't helping,' Awen said.

Suddenly I had the beginnings of an idea. I remembered the way Hatch had injected the knowledge of the Welsh language into my head when I'd arrived at Cantref Gwaelod. I pulled out my Slate and opened the search function. 'Piloting,' I typed. 'Ah! It's here. Look. Piloting information nodule. I can inject it.'

'Quickly!' Awen said. Some of those gathered around the craft were waving their own Slates at it.

'What part of my brain deals with piloting?'

'I'll have a rummage,' Awen said. After a few seconds, she re-emerged. 'It's a bit all over the place, but I'd try stapling it right into your motor cortex, at the centre of the top of your head.'

I raised the corner of the Slate onto my cranium, as Hatch had done, and pressed the screen. Once again, I winced at the stabbing pain, as if I'd been poked with a needle. 'Ow!' And just like that, the purpose of the symbols in front of me were suddenly as obvious as the wheel, handbrake, gearstick and pedals of a car.

'Right, um, let's go, I suppose,' I said, and started tapping away as if I'd done it a thousand times.

The *chwyrligwgan* shot up, scattering the crowd of people like bowling pins.

'Don't we need some kind of permission to get out?' I asked.

'Just go through with some of the other crafts.'

'Hmm.' There were a whole line of airlocks and at least one of them would open every few seconds as a fleet of the smaller crafts shot through. But they seemed carefully timed so that each one closed a second or so after. I'd have to time it exactly. I flew in a broad arc around the hangar and counted the seconds between each airlock opening and closing. As soon as the nearest one closed, I accelerated, counting the seconds under my breath. By the time I was half-way across the hangar it had opened again, and a line of spaceships, flying in geese formation, were passing through.

'Ooh, it's going to be tight,' I said as we approached.

'Too tight!' Awen warned. 'Stop!'

Oh God, she's right, I thought. But I was going too fast to stop. Another second and we'd be through ... But no sooner had those words flashed through my mind than the airlock closed with a thump. I screamed and veered to the left, desperate to avoid a head-on collision. Then the next airlock along opened and swallowed my craft whole. The *chwyrligwgan* hit the wall of the tunnel, sending the craft into a tailspin, but the tug of the airlock had me in its grip and I was sucked backwards and spat out in a belch of bubbles into the sea.

'Woo, we did it!'

'You almost killed us!' Awen said.

'I never knew flying could be this exciting.'

'Well, imagine sitting where I'm sitting. It'll take a while to clean off the inside of your head.'

'Don't be gross, Awen.'

The ship had its own pre-set route to the surface which I could activate on the menu, so I lay back and looked through the glass. As the huge skyscrapers floated past like lost undersea monoliths, I wondered whether I'd ever see the place again.

'I'm sure you'll be welcomed back to a hero's reception,' Awen said.

'And you?'

'Oh, I'll be long gone by then. Job done. But don't worry, I'll let you get all the credit.'

We broke the surface ten minutes later and I followed Awen's instructions in aiming straight up towards orbit. Soon we were above the clouds and all I could see was a vast expanse of blue sky which slowly darkened until it become black, and then the sky was filled by thousands of stars like a tapestry of diamonds. I looked through the transparent floor and saw the Earth like a blue, speckled egg underneath me.

'Wow, look at that view,' I said.

'That's what we're here to defend,' said Awen.

'It looks so ... untouched from up here, as if we haven't ruined it at all.'

I took the straps off one by one and felt myself float up from the floor of the craft. It felt strange, like being underwater but not wet. I closed my eyes but suddenly felt as if I was falling and flailed to grab one of the straps again.

'There's the dragon ship,' Awen said. 'Concentrate.'

I pulled at the strap to catapult myself up to the side of the craft and peered out at the spaceship. I'd imagined a sleek metal cone, perfectly formed and quivering like mercury. Instead, it looked organic, like a giant piece of mouldy meat or a large pimpled tongue.

'Wow, that's ugly,' I said.

'It's wetware.'

'What's that?'

'It's like hardware, which you would build a computer out of. But wetware is biological matter. Rather than thousands of circuits you can have millions of neurons. The dragon ship is like one huge brain.'

I paused. 'We're doomed, aren't we?'

'Don't worry, humanity has a secret weapon.'

'What?'

'The two of us,' she said. 'We'll be fine. I've done this before. I just need to get in close and I can do my thing.'

I steered the ship as close as I could to the huge, blubbering mass. Close up, it looked like a giant Manhattan-sized maggot.

'It does!' said Awen. 'But it's bigger than Manhattan.'

I found a spacesuit rolled into a ball in a small drawer at the side of the ship, and a kind of helmet which I could pull up out of it like a hoodie and zip over my head. It felt too flimsy to be wearing to go into space, especially into a ship full of dragons. Thankfully, there was a gun too, which I took at Awen's advice.

'Now open the door,' Awen said.

'Are you sure I'm going to be able to breathe?'

'If you can't breathe then I can't breathe. I'm sure.'

I pressed the button on the ceiling and the door slid open with a hiss as all the air inside evacuated into the vacuum of space. Beyond, there was nothing between me and the dragon ship but complete emptiness. I felt a chill down my spine, an overwhelming feeling of freedom but also of smallness. I was a dot in the middle of an infinite universe.

'Look at the Earth,' said Awen. 'It looks so fragile ... Like a bubble of air. Like it could pop so easily.'

I pushed away out of the door and spun freely in the emptiness. I could feel the powerful mass of the ship pulling me in.

'I'm going to take control of your body now, Rees,' said Awen. 'Just for a short time. Only until we get inside the ship.'

'If you really have to,' I said, remembering the uncanny feeling when Awen had used my body to knock Brân unconscious. It had felt like being a glove someone was trying to wriggle their hand into.

'Don't worry,' Awen said. 'It's just for this tricky bit. You'll have yourself back in no time.'

I nodded blissfully. I was lying on a blanket of stars, my limbs loose and dangling. What a view, I thought. The solar system all around me, panoramic and perfect. I had the world literally at my feet. For the first time in my life, I felt some kind of peace. That there wasn't some greener grass elsewhere that I was missing out on.

I felt my body go numb. I tried to swing my arm but failed. Awen was in control now. I tried to say 'Remember to breathe,' but I couldn't move my mouth.

'Don't worry,' Awen said. 'Trust me.'

I watched my own hand extend in front of me and grasp the side of the dragon ship. My arm swung the rest of my body around and I scaled the side of the ship until I reached a large, pulsing crater in the ship's skin.

I had no mouth to protest as Awen dragged my body in through this uninviting hole. As I entered, the ship's gravity grabbed me like a hand and I was dragged down a slippery tube covered in dark-green goo.

It felt like I'd just been flushed down a clogged toilet.

I landed on a soft carpet of algae-like plants which shone metallic-green in the darkness. All around me was a murky, jungle-like swamp. It didn't look like any spaceship I'd ever seen in a film or TV show. And I was grateful that, inside my suit, I couldn't smell it.

'Can I have my body back, now?' I thought.

'No.'

'What do you mean?'

'It would be easier to let me complete the rest of the work. You don't know the way.'

'It's my body!'

'I'm sorry, Rees.'

'It's my body!'

I fought to regain control. It was like trying to sit up in a coffin.

'It. Is. Mine!'

I could feel Awen trying to hold her grip, but I strained against her, wildly. I focused on my arms, starting with my fingers. *Wiggle*, I thought. Just *wiggle*. I aimed all my will and fury into the tips of my fingers, and just when I thought I had nothing left inside of me, my finger twitched.

I was exhausted. I couldn't keep it up. It was impossible.

'Huh, no one's ever been able to do that before,' Awen said, an edgy tone to her voice.

Suddenly my entire body jerked. I curled my hand into a fist and held it in front of me. I was back in control.

'OK, you drive,' Awen said, sulkily. 'If you're going to be such a baby. But don't blame me if something goes wrong.'

'Don't you ever dare do that again,' I said. 'Or I'll throw myself out of this spaceship, and down to the Earth.'

'You'd die.'

'Yes, and you too.'

I took out my gun and stumbled on through the curtain of creepers that hung from the knotted branches above.

'Right, I go, you tell me what direction,' I said.

'Straight on,' she said, 'to the ship's brain.'

CHAPTER 12

THE END

My visor was steamed up by the moist air which hung heavy and thick, disturbed only by a sudden breeze which rattled through the tunnels. It felt like I was inside the tired lung of a giant old creature taking its last breath.

The tunnels were clearly made for much larger animals, and I crept through them like some feeble insect. This was made harder by the fact there was little gravity inside the ship, which would have been great if I'd wanted to bounce around like some video game character but was not ideal for sneaking. I had to walk bent almost double to stop myself hovering up towards the ceiling. I did not fancy being spotted by a dragon and burnt to a crisp.

'Is this what it's like on their planet?' I asked.

'Yes. Dragons can't see much,' replied Awen. 'The sky on their planet is too full of volcano smog, so they don't get much sunlight. They depend on their noses.'

We came to what looked like a giant cage rising from the mist, stained green by the marsh water.

'Not a cage,' said Awen. 'Look closer.'

I peered through the fog, straining my eyes. No, not a cage. The ribcage of a skeleton.

'A dead dragon?' I asked. 'Why haven't they buried it?'

'They've been at war for a long time,' said Awen.

'With who?'

'Who knows? They're always making war with someone.'

I heard a noise behind me and dived in slow-motion behind one of the creeping plants. It sounded like an animal sensing the air, a snotty sniffing, and then there was a loud crunch, as if it had crushed a tree or some alien plant beneath its feet. It was breathing heavily, then coughing.

I peeped around the side of the bush. A dragon, wandering around, wounded-looking. It nuzzled its great nose into the ground as if hoping to find something to eat. Its skin was green and yellow, unlike the crimson red of the dragon I'd seen on the screen in Cantref Gwaelod.

'It's sick,' whispered Awen. 'But it's not safe.'

I passed it by, staying close to the walls, my heart thudding. At one point it froze and cocked its head, as if hearing something, and I thought I was really dead this time. But then it let out a huge sneeze, coating the floor with thick, stringy snot, and I breathed with relief.

Once clear of the dragon, I moved on, soon reaching the end of the tunnel and climbing through an overhang in the wall. I could see lights shining on the other end and headed for them, dodging the thick branches that had invaded the passage.

I was not prepared for what I found.

The centre of the ship was hollowed out, like the cavern of a volcano, and it was as infested with dragons as a cave with bats. They clung to every wall, and hundreds filled the sky, flapping around on broad leathery wings. Hanging in the middle, supported by vein-like towers, was a huge pulsing mass.

'The ship's brain,' explained Awen. 'The control centre. If you can get me there, past the dragons, we can destroy this ship, and you can go home a hero.'

'But it's surrounded by those things!' I said, in a terrified whisper. 'I'll be gulped down!'

'They won't eat you. They don't know where you've been. They may burn you alive in your suit like a banana in some foil wrapping, though, so be careful.'

'Oh, thanks for that,' I said, frowning. 'How do I get there?'

'Climb down one of those brain stems.'

I looked at the vein-like structures that slipped down towards the ship's brain. With a big enough leap, I calculated, I could get from where I was to the nearest one, some twenty feet away. It was difficult to get my head around which way was down because all the gravity pulled towards the centre of the ship.

I took a deep breath and leapt, hanging in the air for

a moment before slowly starting my descent towards the stem. The jump seemed to take forever, so I had plenty of time to worry I was aiming in the wrong direction. I landed with a bump – the 'brain stem' as Awen had called it was harder than it looked – then slipped, and just about managed to hold on by my fingertips.

I looked down. It was a good half a mile to the centre of the cavern and if I fell the whole way I'd no doubt be picked off by a dragon like a seagull grabbing a stray chip.

'So don't fall,' said Awen.

I started climbing down carefully, hoping I wouldn't be noticed. Every now and then I'd have to freeze and hang on tight as a dragon flew past, its massive wings sending gusts of wind that almost knocked me off my perch.

As I approached the brain, a larger problem presented itself. An enormous dragon was hanging bat-like on the very stem I was grappling down. I tried to squeeze past it, but its wings were like a rugged cloak covering the entirety of the stem.

'You're going to have to climb on the dragon,' said Awen.

You've got to be joking, I thought, too scared to even whisper.

'Can you think of any alternatives?' said Awen.

I could not.

'Then get going!'

I bloody hate you, I thought.

'I know for a fact that you don't.'

I gently placed one shaky foot on the dragon's snout. I could smell my own sweat inside the suit and my own gasping breath was steaming up the visor. I was just about to take another careful step when the dragon opened its mouth wide and fire blasted out from it. I pulled back, shielding myself from the heat with my arm.

The dragon shook itself in its sleep and started snoring.

'Go on,' Awen said.

I placed my foot on its snout once more, and then the other. Again sparks erupted from its nostrils but I was quicker this time and swung swiftly down its neck, dropping to its scaly but softer belly. A large claw appeared and tried to scratch me away, as if I was a bed bug. I scurried down and found myself hanging off the dragon's tail, which swung back and forth like the pendulum of a clock. As the tail approached the stem I let go and launched myself through the air and grabbed on to one of the big veins.

'Oh God,' I said, my voice trembling. 'You – you know, after this, I think I'll happily go back to weeding.'

'Well done,' Awen said.

'I don't look forward to climbing back up there.'

'I wouldn't worry too much about it,' she said, in a

quiet, strange voice.

'There's not going to be a return journey, is there?' I said.

'No time to think about that now,' she said. 'Come on, you're so close.'

She was right. I concentrated on placing one foot in front of the other, and after some careful grappling, I eventually fell down on to the brain itself. It was like standing on a water-filled bouncy castle that was also covered with a thick layer of gooey washing-up liquid. Under the see-through surface were harder veins that seemed to thrum with electro-magnetic energy.

'This is disgusting,' I said. 'If this is the brain, I wouldn't like to see the other end.'

'How do you think we got in?'

'Ugh. OK, what do we do now?' I trod across the brain, which seemed to be about the size of a house.

'Rees!'

It wasn't Awen's voice, but a man's. I turned in surprise and there was Hatch, in a spacesuit just like mine, bouncing across the brain towards me.

'Hatch!' I laughed with relief. 'What on earth are you doing here? Jesus, am I glad to see you.'

He stopped and raised his gun and pointed it at my head.

'Put your hands up,' he said.

I took a step back and slowly raised my hands. 'What the hell? Hatch man, I'm about to destroy the brain and save the Earth.'

'Who am I talking to?' Hatch asked. 'You, Rees, or that thing in your head?'

'Don't listen to him,' Awen said. 'He's lost it.'

'You're talking to me, Hatch,' I said. 'What – what are you doing?'

'The dragons aren't the bad guys here, for once,' Hatch said. 'They pose no threat to us. They're after a terrorist that came to Earth two days ago. A terrorist from a race of parasitic aliens with the ability to infect and take over any organic matter.' He kept the gun trained on me the whole time. 'Including this ship. Including humans. Including you.'

'Hatch, the dragons are the bad guys,' I said. 'I saw her memories. They destroyed her family. Destroyed her planet.'

'They destroyed a terrorist base. She, as you call it, was the only one that managed to escape. Since then it has been wreaking havoc across the galaxy, taking control of dragon ships, destroying worlds. It has to be stopped.'

'Is this true?' I whispered.

'Well, a bit,' Awen said. 'They call me a terrorist. I'd call it fighting for my people.'

A shock went down my spine and I felt my body jerk

like a marionette on a string as Awen took it over.

'You've done your part, Rees,' she said. 'Soon I won't need you any more. Soon I'll be able to jump from your tiny brain into the ship's brain. Destroy the dragons. Destroy Earth too. I didn't really like it there.'

'Rees? Is everything OK?' Hatch asked.

'She's taking ... ov—' I could feel my words slur as I lost control of my jaw and the rest of my body. Transfixed with horror, I lifted my gun and pointed it at Hatch.

'Put the gun down!' Hatch barked.

'Shoot, if you want to,' I heard my own voice come out, cold and gruff. 'You will only kill your friend. You won't damage me. I have found a new host. A much more powerful host.'

'No!' I tried to yell, but my mouth wouldn't move. She had complete control. I felt myself reach out a hand and touch the surface of the ship's brain.

'One more step and I shoot!' Hatch said. 'I'll shoot you to pieces. I know you're in there somewhere.'

'Awen,' I thought, 'before you say goodbye.'

'Yes?'

'I'd just like to say thank you.'

'Thank you?' she asked. 'Why?'

'You told me to stop running away. To stand firm. To face my fears.'

'I did.'

'And you told me to release myself from the shackles that bound me.'

'I did.'

'So, that's what I'm going to do. I'm releasing myself from you.'

All I needed was one arm and one finger. The arm to grab the muzzle and pull, and the finger to shoot. That would be enough. But I felt like I was wrestling with a boa constrictor. I strained with every sinew of my being for control. My left arm began to shake.

'Stop fighting!' Awen said. 'It's hopeless. Your body is mine now.'

'It's mine,' I thought.

I focused my entire being on just the very tip of my finger. My jaw and neck tightened until I feared I was going to pass out with the effort. My temples throbbed. Just the one finger. Wiggle, damn you. Wiggle.

Yes! I felt it. I could do it.

'Stop!' my own mouth shouted, a deep guttural roar, and I couldn't tell if it was me or Awen screaming. No, it was her. She couldn't control it. She was throwing everything at me now. Horrible visions. My family drowning. The charred remains of an alien corpse. A dragon, flaming.

'Let go!' I screamed, and it was definitely me this time. I felt my left arm slowly lift and I grabbed hold of the barrel of the gun and pulled it under my chin.

'What are you doing?' Awen shrieked. 'You'll kill us both.'

'Saving the world.'

Now all I needed to do was curl my finger.

Curl, finger. *Curl*.

'No!' She was fighting back. I felt my right hand try to pull away, taking the gun with it. 'Nooooo!'

Pow! A flash of white light and a deafening screech. I felt something dark and sticky crawl out of my nose.

I fell to the floor and heard Hatch shout 'Stop!' before three further gunshots rang out.

Then, a deathly silence.

'Rees!' Hatch ran over and leant next to me. 'Oh no, there's a hole in your spacesuit.'

I raised a hand to my face and could feel my glove on my cheek. Not a good sign. Part of my visor was shattered.

'I tried to kill myself, and I think I missed,' I said.

Hatch lifted me up to a sitting position. 'Well, the good news is I got that thing.'

'Awen? She's dead?' I wiped my visor clean with my free hand – a hand that was now my own – and saw a large streak of silver-green goo on the floor. 'Was that her?'

'Yes.'

Wow. I suddenly felt lonely, in my brain all by myself. I'd seen her thoughts, felt her emotions. Anger. Betrayal.

I'd understood what had driven her to it. Looking at that streak on the floor, I realised that I'd lived inside her just as much as she'd lived inside me. It was like looking at my own body in the Elimination Department. As if a part of me had died too.

I coughed. I could feel the air become muggier. It smelt sulphuric, like volcanic ash. 'I'm losing air.'

'Let's get you back to the ship.'

Hatch lifted me up.

'I don't think I've got enough oxygen,' I said, coughing again.

'You'll be OK.'

I took another breath and felt hot, dry air burn the inside of my lungs. 'I can't breathe.'

That's when I saw it approach – a huge black dragon that unfolded its giant wings like shadows and landed with a thump on one of the brain stems. It was Drachfolga Bolorembus, the Emperor of Dragons.

It roared and I closed my eyes.

'We're getting on its back,' Hatch said.

'Its back? But ...'

Drachfolga squatted down and Hatch pushed me up its hot, scaly side. I felt something nudging my ribs – it was Drachfolga's snout, helping to edge me up. I collapsed onto the dragon's back and Hatch scrambled up beside me.

The last thing I remember before losing consciousness was soaring through the sky, surrounded by a thousand creatures that amassed in a black cloud and blotted out my view until I could see nothing but darkness.

CHAPTER 13

HOME

I awoke coughing up black ash. It felt as though my lungs had been filled with hot cement. The sky above the *chwyrligwgan* was an azure blue and below, the sea sparkled like a mirror, inches from the skimming craft. Near my feet was my scrunched up spacesuit, covered in grey soot.

The memory of what had happened on the dragon ship came back to me like a hammer to the gut.

I ran my hands across my face. 'I made a mess of things.'

'No, you didn't,' Hatch said. He was laid down next to me, steering the ship.

'I let her in. I let her in to Cantref Gwaelod and I almost let her destroy the Earth. Everyone here is going to blame me, aren't they? I screwed up.'

Hatch shook his head. 'You can never blame one person for anything. And anyway, all's well that ends well.'

'Because you stopped me.'

'You did what you thought was right, and in the end, you saved us.'

I pulled off my straps and sat up, watching where the

blue of the sea and the horizon faded into one another. I could see clouds like jellyfish trailing rain tentacles beneath them.

I thought of Awen and felt a pang of something – loss? Maybe she'd left a little part of herself behind in me. How did I even know she *was* the bad guy? *She* certainly didn't seem to think that. She thought she was fighting for something. Perhaps I'd made the wrong choice. Perhaps I should have been fighting for her too. I'd probably never know.

'Where are we going?' I asked.

'Twelve years ago, I told you that your home is where you choose to make it.' He looked at me through the corner of his eye. 'It's true that we've never let anyone leave Cantref Gwaelod, but, like I've said before, that's only because no one has ever *wanted* to leave.'

'Brân said I'd have to leave through an airlock,' I said.

Hatch smiled, his crow's feet multiplying. 'A joke I like to crack once in a while, after a beer or two. Well, here we are. And what to do?' He drummed his fingers on his thigh, thinking. 'I trust you, Rees, so I'm giving you a choice.'

I blew air out. 'Home isn't just a place. Home is people.'

He nodded.

It was night by the time he dropped me off in the park in Cardiff. I could see the lights out in the street beyond the park gate. I breathed in the night air. Autumn would soon be winter and my breath was already coming out in puffs of steam.

'Difficult choice?' Hatch asked.

'I just don't want to hurt anyone again.'

He kicked a dry leaf and sent it tumbling. 'It wasn't your fault, you know.'

'What?'

He crossed his arms and looked down. 'The crash,' he said.

I felt my stomach tighten into a ball. I thought back to that night on the edge of the lake. The sudden lurch of the car as it spun on the road. The weightlessness as it flipped.

I shook my head. 'It was my fault,' I said. 'I was having a stupid argument with my little sister. Dad told me to shut up, that I was distracting him, and then we crashed.' I wiped my eyes with my sleeve.

Hatch shook his head. 'That lake is one of the entrances to Cantref Gwaelod. Your dad was distracted by a *chwyrligwgan*. Didn't know what he'd seen, and crashed the car.' Hatched looked at me with his piercing eyes.

I stared at him open mouthed. 'You're just saying this to make me feel better.'

'Why do you think I chose you, Rees? Out of everyone? Kept an eye on you all those years?' Hatch looked up at the sky. 'I know what it's like to feel guilty. And what no one tells you about Cantref Gwaelod is that that's the heaviest burden. Because the longer you live, the more regrets you have.' He smiled sadly. 'Hey, did you ever wonder why everyone calls me Hatch?'

I was still stunned. 'No.'

'I'm Seithenyn.' He leaned forward. 'You forget to close off one damn hangar door, and everyone takes the piss out of you for the rest of your life.'

He chuckled, turned and wandered back in the direction of the stone circle.

'You've still got your Slate,' he called back. 'I'll be waiting. Whenever you're ready. You don't even have to be a weeder!'

I watched him go and laughed to myself. A laugh of pure, clean joy. It suddenly felt as if a great weight had lifted from my shoulders. I made my way to the shelter, still laughing, my shoes crunching across the dry leaves on the grass.

Everything was as I'd left it. The same police sirens in the distance. The same rust-coloured sky that blocked out the stars.

As I crossed the street, I could already see her standing at the open door, in her vest and pyjama bottoms. She was standing under a street lamp, framed by light, having a smoke. Looking for all the world like the femme fatale in a black and white movie. But one wearing faded pyjamas.

'Hi, Megan.'

The cigarette fell from her mouth. I saw her cheeks redden.

'You snuck out again and left me,' she said, her voice husky. 'You dick.'

I put my hands in my pockets.

'I'm sorry,' I said. 'I've treated you like shit, I really have. But I've learnt my lesson. Genuinely.'

'You're never going again?' She took out another cigarette and lit it. 'I've heard that one before.'

'No, I *am* going away again. But because I think I belong somewhere now, not to run away from anything. But I'd like to bring you with me. If you want to go. Because I love you.'

I wrapped my arms around her. She tensed at first, resistant, but I kissed her head all over, the temple, forehead, crown, the spot between her eyebrows, and she laughed, pushing me away. But with a smile.

'So, where the hell did you go?'

I paused. 'Megan?'

'Yes?'

'Did you ever hear the legend of Cantref Gwaelod?'

111

Congratulations on completing a 2020 Quick Read.

The Quick Reads project, with bite-sized books, is designed to get readers back into the swing of reading, and reading for pleasure. So we sincerely hope you enjoyed this book.

Got an opinion?

Your feedback can make this project better. Now you've read one of the Quick Reads series visit www.readingwales.org.uk or Twitter @quickreads2020 to post your feedback.

→ Why did you choose this book?

→ What did you like about it?

→ What do you think of the Quick Reads series?

→ Which Quick Reads would you like to see in the future?

What next?

Now that you've finished one Quick Read – got time for another?

Look out for the other title in the 2020 Quick Reads series – *Dogs for Life* by Alison Stokes.